GOLDFIELD:

An Anthology of Western Superstition

Devan Arntson

GOLDFIELD

ISBN: 978-0-578-34490-4

For

Grandpa Dave,
Who took me to Goldfield and Superstition Mountain growing up.
Thank you for the cover photo.

And

Grandpa Arntson,
Who showed me a few western movies, borrowed me a few books,
and got me hooked on the genre forever. I still need to return those
to you.

GOLDFIELD

GOLDFIELD

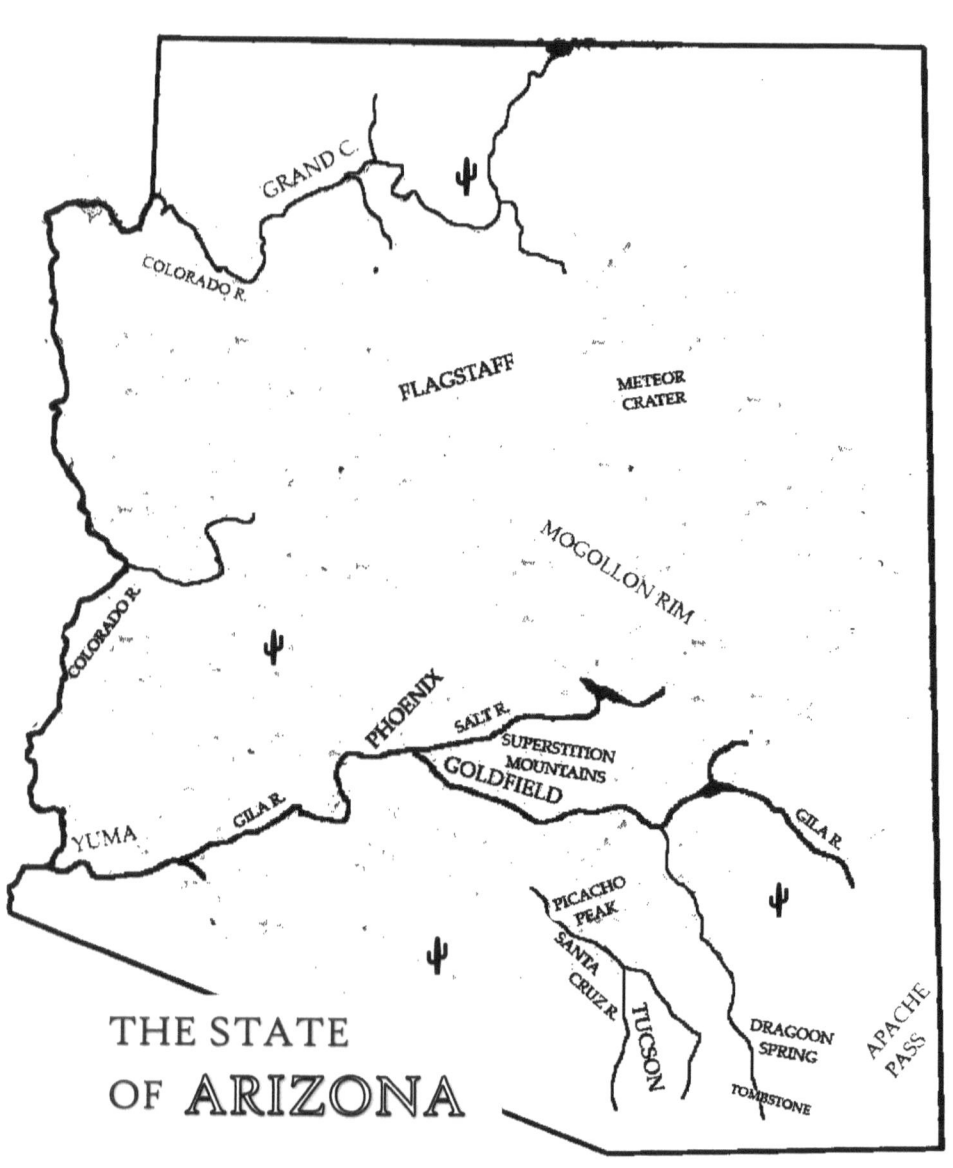

THE STATE
OF ARIZONA

Opening Regards

Now, it's been said that superstitions will always remain preeminent over facts, that a rumor will linger far after its owner is dead and gone. Some have even said that legends sell more papers than facts. It makes sense then, why there are so many legends about the short lived, yet explosive, era of the Wild West. But I am here to testify that truth is stranger than fiction and legends are closer than you think.

This is the story, as orderly as I can tell, about the events of Superstition Mountain and the gold mine therein. This story has only three characters: the godforsaken mine, every fool that died goin' after it, and me. In the Southwest of what is now Arizona, lies a mountain. It's not a mountain in the most traditional sense of the word. There's no triangular peak, certainly no snow. It looked kind of like a razorback hog, all jagged with stacks and piles of rock. It was full of thorns and cactus as if the ground were never meant to be lived on. It was quiet like all other plateaus in the desert. It sits, unabated by the scorching heat.

Year after year, millennia after millennia, it sat untouched. Until one day, these three characters showed up. Since then, this mountain didn't hear the shifting of sand nor the rattling of vipers. It only heard gunshots. It wasn't yellow with sandstone; it was dyed red with blood—soaked deep to its foundations. Yet below the red and rocky surface was gold, more gold than mankind was ever meant to see. Now, other mines were later drilled into those rocks but have little mystery in the shadow of what has become known as the *Lost Dutchman's gold mine.*

There are some though, that claim it only superstition. That the mine never really existed, that it only served to draw people into that ghost town. They say people are drawn to the things they can't have. It becomes obsession, endless chasing after thin air. I am here to testify, though, that the entirety of the story is true. Many different testimonies have come forward about the following events. It would seem historians and local folk would all disagree on what it was that actually took place. However, it is my sole responsibility to put to rest the audacious idea that these are all just *superstitions.* When, in fact, they are all a part of one story. And all very real.

Though there have been claims that there are conflicting narratives to disprove my plot, I am here to assure that there are no such conundrums. Actions of each of the persons involved cannot contradict one another if all actions were taken out of the avarice of gold. This testimony of mine follows through history, suppose all those cowboys and Indians are my witnesses. There may be a lot of names to follow, and quite a few places, too. Just remember, there's only three of us in this story: the gold mine, those who died, and me.

I have personally undergone the most tedious task of researching and preparing these reports to assure that this is the most authoritative and thorough testimony for what has all taken place concerning the Lost Dutchman's gold. To ward anyone from ever seeking that mine. And I suppose as a defense of all that I have done, which will be explained in due time.

Part 1
The Mine

GOLDFIELD

The Gold Rush, 1850

Miguel Peralta is where our story begins. After weeks of foot travel through the unforgiving land, he had finally reached the top of a lone mountain. From this height, the Mexican could see the flat horizon in every direction of the compass. He led his whole family through the uncharted mountains that hot day. They would have died of dehydration if it weren't for the Salt River barely trickling by on the North base of the mountain.

The Peralta clan was nearing a hundred strong. They lost members constantly, but they seemed to get on alright. It was hard life in the West, but no one expected it to go easy. They'd been all over Alta California before Mexico ceded it to these United States. They wandered everywhere, looking for a place to settle. Some have even claimed they'd started walking from Mexico City. Now, I don't think anyone knew where they were originally from, suppose it doesn't matter too much. What matters is where they stopped.

His family had followed Miguel to California in the gold rush of '49. Men of all stripes fled to the piece of country in hopes of finding fortune. Men dug into the old dirt, some striking it rich, while others left empty handed, if'n they left at all. Where Miguel had started digging, all of the men in the area were starving. No one within a week's ride had found any such gold. Brawls broke out in the pop-up towns, people started shooting each other for what scraps of food they could afford or find. Everyone watched their back, careful not to find a knife in it.

This is where I say that evil was alive and well from the very beginning of this plot. Men are cruel to each other. Men do wicked, cheating things. Things that have dire consequences. The devil needn't interfere, but he *did*. That wicked creature saw an opportunity for great evil, and he took it. See, some of the men camped next to Miguel devised a scheme to get at his money, which he still had from when he arrived. The Mexican's large family was also eating up too much food for the town to support. So, they couldn't just kill him off like ol' McGee, they needed to get rid of the whole clan. And if they could take his money while they were at it, all the better. The miners got together and forged this deed to a claim, far to the East. Far enough for Miguel to never be a problem again. They drew up a map with it and everything. They told him this mine was the real deal, no more mounds of dirt like they were digging in, but a real mine full of gold. Miguel didn't know the region any better, so he fell for it. He bought the claim on the high hopes that he would lead his family to glorious riches.

The entire Peralta clan followed Miguel in his shameless pursuits. I guess he was somewhat of a patriarch in that way. Wherever he'd go, they'd go. Wherever he'd stay—well, you know the saying...

When he gambled himself into debt and was thrown out of towns, his *familia* went with him. When Miguel fell asleep fishing off a raft on the Colorado and drifted downstream, the rest of the Peralta's were on the shore when he woke. So, when Miguel was promised a gold mine that had no end to it, he couldn't pass up the offer. He spent what little he had on those scraps of paper and took his entire family with him.

The grouping of "crooked topped" mountains lay just south of a river and a bit east of another. And "river" is a generous term. It was all wildland back in that age, years before any other settlement was built. Lord knows how Miguel's wandering feet found the region, but it matched his map perfectly.

"Look around," Miguel called to his family, all of em on the summit of the mount. "The mine's up here somewhere."

His family spread out over the ridge, searching everywhere for the foretold entrance. People say the only reason that coot ever found the mine was the fact that his family was large enough to cover every square foot of the rock. Whether that holds up, or if the devil again placed it into the world, doesn't matter. The principle is: he followed a fake map to a fake mine and *found it*.

The cave was in a little pocket on the topside of the mountain. It borrowed deep into the rock. The cave was small, too small for a grown man to crawl through, but they knew this had to be the entrance. There wasn't a doubt about it. Miguel took his youngest nephew, and holding him at the ankles, lowered him down into the crevasse. The little boy's lantern reflected off of every wall. Light so fiercely illuminated out from below, that the family forgot it was dusk. It was like pure sunlight had beaconed from the heart of the mountain.

"What do you see?" An older man asked. He was covering his eyes from the bright light. Yet, he peeked between his fingers. The young boy refused to answer, that or he couldn't find any words to describe a sight that God damned beautiful. As Miguel pulled the kid out, in his hands was a rock.

"The stone was bigger than a water canteen," Miguel wrote in his journal. "It was big and shiny. It was gold." Some of the men immediately took their picks and swung at the cave, trying to open it wide enough to see the vein for themselves. All night, they chipped at the rock, making it ever so larger with each swing.

They swung all evening, all night, and into the next morning. The sounds of iron cutting down rock echoed over the empty desert. Slowly, the entrance began to take shape. At dawn, the rocks fell through and the morning sun reflected off the cavern wall. A light so strong, it was said to have blinded the great Apache archer, Alchesay, causing him to miss his first shot ever. Over a hundred miles away, the old archer was routinely shooting a prickly pear off of his apprentice's head. Yet the blinding light wavered his aim and he fired straight into the young man's thigh (It's relevant, I promise).

Down in the flats, the Peralta family started to dig in; cutting down the hazardous cholla cacti and planting what seeds and roots they brought with them. Their little Miguel had finally struck it rich. And real dirty rich at that. They were quick to landscape around the mine, concealing it enough so that it would not be visible to an unsuspecting eye. Or seen from the reflecting sun. Though, as far as they knew, they were alone. They could've been the only people in the whole territory for all they knew. Miguel and his brothers and cousins and uncles dug out borrows of sacred gold and loaded them into crates. Those crates were then taken and buried back into the mountain for safe keeping. Logically. They worked all day, with the adrenaline of riches keeping them going. They would only come down from the mine to sleep in the camp. But as many days as they would work, the cave would only get deeper. There seemed no end to the gold. A couple of the miners had even fashioned golden plates and bowls and "goldware" for themselves. For as long as they mined, the mountain would provide.

The Salt River winded along the north side of the mountain, but the walk to it was far and rugged. If the collected water didn't spill out from the hike, it would evaporate from the heat. Some historians wondered why they didn't just build their camp next to the river, but I'm not here to justify their actions. I'm only here to report what they did...

Eventually, a well was dug down in camp, providing a more suitable source of water. They used the water to irrigate some vegetables planted outside their tents, but farming was hard in such an arid place. So, the Peralta's took to hunting. And by hunting, I mean letting their children go and catch snakes. Again, I'm not here to justify...

Their camp wasn't much more than a field of tents. Mainly posts and canvas to provide any sort of respite from the sun. They did manage to pull together enough lumber to make three shacks near the base of the mountain. One was for Miguel, the others for his brother and sister and their families.

They were all a tight-knit bunch. The family loved to dance together and play music at night. They would tell stories around the blazing campfires and have big feasts whenever they brought in enough food. Times were finally turning out for the best for this clan. Poor Miguel, though, he missed out. He was so proud that he had actually struck gold, that he worked himself harder than the rest. His tent was set up at the mouth of the mine, which wasn't a bad way to hide a hole in the ground. While his family was singing and dancing below, he would be working. Sometimes he'd be digging for so long and was so far back in the mine, he didn't know if it was day or night. Sometimes he would get into such a rhythm that he lost sight of ore vein and was just swinging recklessly at the rock. It was like his eyes were glazed over and nothing went through his mind anymore.

He wasn't the only one, though. Old age started to take some of the miners, or at least their memories. Some of the old crows started to forget where the mine was. Even if they spotted the tent from the base of the mountain, they couldn't reckon how to get up there. The ground was so arid and harsh, that the heavily traveled path didn't make any impression. It was Miguel's brother, Pablo, that came up with the idea to give each miner a map to lead them up the mountain. Yet there was nothing in the region to produce any paper and the family couldn't afford to give up any scraps of fabric.

"Stones," Miguel thought aloud from on top of the mountain.

"Stones?" Pablo turned. He was thinner than his brother. Same black hair and tan skin. He wore a white long-sleeve and a wide brim hat to keep himself out of the sun.

"Why it's our only resource out here. Unless you want to scribble a map onto a cactus," Miguel shook his head. "We place way stones along the trail, carved in them is a piece of the map."

"So, if they get lost along the way, they just find one of these stones? Wouldn't it be better to mark the trail with cairns or signs or something?"

"No," Miguel rebuked. "They need to be discrete. We can't afford others finding the mine."

"Look over the desert, *hermano*, there are no others!" Pablo pointed across the flats. The land was uncivilized except for Miguel's own family. Nothing else even came into view, nothing but rugged arid desert surrounded their lone mountains.

"Just trust me on this. When people hear how much gold we're hauling out of this rock, they'll come flocking. There'll be people here one day and they will come after our gold."

"You're right," Pablo nodded and stood. "We'll play it safe."

Miguel grunted as he got up and went back towards the mine.

Pablo called after him. "Brother, give it up for tonight." He saw Miguel open his mouth, about to protest. "Please."

Eventually he nodded and starting walking across the mountaintop. The next day, two worked back up the mountain and carved into various rocks, indicating turns and landmarks in their crude maps. The stones were stood, with the map facing outward as subtle guides to the mouth of the cave. With the stones, the miners were able to continue going into the mountain and bringing out crates of raw gold ore. The work never ceased. The song of metal chiming never stopped.

~

"Miguel!" Pablo called into the mineshaft. "Brother, where are you?" Miguel kept swinging his pickaxe, not choosing to hear anything other than the ring of gold nuggets falling onto the ground. "Miguel, it's time to choose..." At this, the determined man dropped his axe, wiped his sweat, and started up toward the outside world. Miguel put on his sombrero as he left the cave. His eyes burned at the sun, as he emerged from the dark mineshaft. He walked with his brother down the rock to the tent city below.

"I will go!" A young man spoke up in the crowd, which gathered at the fire rings.

"No, let it be me," One of the elders got up. "I've lived long enough, if I should be ambushed, it's less of a waste."

"No, let Jose go!" The young man's mother waved her arms and pleaded.

"Why not both? Insurance that they come back with supplies!"

"Why don't a lot of us go?" Another cried out.

"Then you'll never come back!"

"Why does everyone wish to leave?" Miguel asked his brother, standing behind the crowd.

"Miguel, our family... they're getting bored. We've been out here for months. There isn't a lot for them to do, they're restless. All this gold does nothing if it can't feed our family. We're still living just as we were," Pablo replied. Miguel then walked over to the boy who was offering to go.

"Jose will make the trip," Miguel's family silenced to listen to him. "Take only a few bags, that will be enough. Go east, back to civilization. When you reach a town, circle around and enter from the South, so they do not know where you came from. Then when you return, leave in the early morning, so you are not followed back."

The young lad stocked the saddle bags on the family mule and was given a sombrero from his mother. Bags full of gold ore along with water and food. His mother kissed him farewell and hit the mule on the rump to start walking. The teen whistled to himself as he strutted east. He relaxed at the thought of leaving the desolate mountain camp.

"Do we know for sure there is a town?" Miguel's brother asked him after the people cleared out.

"Pablo, the map led us here. If the map says there is a town out east, then there is," His brother scoffed. It wasn't a bad assumption either. A lot of miners had come up from Mexico into the region. Surely there was a town somewhere.

Miguel nodded and started to hike back up the mountain.

"Woah. Take a break, would you? Who'll dig your gold when your crippled? At least for tonight."

"Alright, *mi hermano*. You win," Miguel took off his hat and went to where the others were gathering. The family stared at Miguel as he sat down among them, expecting him to have something important to say. He hadn't joined their festivities since they first struck gold. Eventually though, the Peraltas tuned up their guitars and started to play.

~

Each day, more and more of the Peralta's called it quits in the mine. Soon, only Miguel dug. It was not for the lack of wealth, but the opposite. The cave went on so far, that it almost didn't matter anymore. There was no one near enough to sell to. No matter how much gold Miguel drug out at the end of the day, everyone was still living like poor villagers.

"There's been talk down in camp," Miguel's brother sat on a boulder in the mine. He tossed to himself an ore of gold bigger than a fattened rat.

"That so?" Miguel swung as his brother kept watch on him. "What of?"

"Of going out to find Jose. It has been weeks; the boy hasn't showed up. We don't want to leave you, we've been following you since papa set you in charge, but we always had a home nearby to go to. We have nothing here, no trees even to build. We were able to put up three houses with the supplies we brought with us, but we have nothing more to build with. We can't right build houses out of the cacti!"

"You've tried?"

"Ci, some of the cousins wanted to make a more secure outhouse. Didn't end well."

"Ah," He thought before swinging again.

"Miguel, I beg you. We have more gold than our generations will ever need. I admire you wanting to provide for the family. You've always stuck out your neck for us, and you've done your job. Now it's time to move on, let them be happy. Take the gold we have and go find a town, let them go and find Jose."

"You're right," He set down the pickaxe. "I just wanted to make father proud. I wanted to prove that I wasn't a deadbeat, that I had what it took to lead the family. You're right, I have done my part. We can take the gold and move on. Sell the deed to a company in the East."

~

Far from the Peralta mine, Jose meandered on his mule. He sat back in the saddle, with the sombrero covering his vision. Dangerously dehydrated, he simply faded in and out sleep. He didn't notice where his mule went, not even when the beast stopped to drink himself, climbing in and out of an old riverbed. If Jose still remembered his appointed task, it didn't mean anything now. His mule, with no given direction, started to go insane and began to walk in circles.

"Look," An Apache warrior pointed across the field.

"But what is he doing?" An elder stepped forward. They peered at the mule who carried Jose along where it roamed. It walked aimlessly around the flat desert.

"Maybe it's a distraction?"

"Maybe he's dead?" The two Indians thought aloud.

"He is one of them," Alchesay came forward, being led by his son. His eyes were shut and painted over. "He is from the people who possess light."

"They don't seem that civilized," His son spoke up. He was a young warrior. Shaved head and bright yellow war paint.

"Don't be fooled, Delshay," Alchesay said. "There are no other peoples around. He has to be with them. Their magic blinded me, who knows what other powers they have?" The other warriors with him shrugged and shook their heads at their once proud archer. "We carry on, ignore their distraction."

Alchesay started forward, with him followed hundreds of native warriors, prepared for war. They walked past Jose and his mule, who didn't seem to notice. Jose was left alone in the sunset, eventually collapsing off the mule and was left to the harsh desert.

~

"I told you, we have enough gold packed. Let's make sure we have room for food."

"Pablo, we can buy more food when we get there with the gold," Miguel continued to stack crates of gold into the covered wagon.

"We won't get there if we don't pack enough food," Pablo unloaded the heavy crate. "We have no idea how far away the town is."

"Then we keep hunting and gathering along the way, you worry too much. A little struggle now, a little starvation, is all worth it when we find civilization again. We've been here a year; we've done just as well as we have before. Eighteen fifty-one will be a great year for our family. I just know it, brother."

The Peralta Massacre, 1851

Alchesay grabbed an arrow from his quiver, he drew his bow and aimed into the sky. The warm wind blew in his hair. Red paint covered his closed eyes and smeared down the sides of his cheeks. He wore a yellow headband and frilled buckskin pants. Alchesay breathed in through his nostrils then released the arrow.

"Come on now, help me load these boxes," Miguel turned to see that his brother lay dead on the sand, with an arrow in his chest. "*Jesus Cristo!*"

Miguel fell back to the ground. He scrambled to his feet and ran to the mountain. Turning back, Miguel saw arrows darting through camp. Peraltas ran away from the invasion, but many were struck down by the arrows, sticking into their calves and backs. Gunshots were heard, too. Black powder smoke filled the dusty air. Arrows and bullets ripped through tents and lodged themselves into the wooden carts. From the outside of camp, Apache fighters whooped and howled as they ran with weapons in hand. The Peraltas were cornered against the base of the mountain and had no weapons to defend themselves. They were outmatched.

"I'm sorry," Miguel cried as he scurried up the mountain, not looking back on his town, being destroyed behind him. Fearing the Apache would follow the stones to his hiding place, he kicked and threw the marked stones off the trail.

Most falling down the mountain side, breaking or landing among the field of other fallen rock and cactus below.

Warriors continued to tear through the camp with axes and spears. Tents were torn down and wagons broken apart. Animals scattered into the wild if they weren't killed by the hailstorm of arrows. The Apache slashed down at their enemy with no remorse. Peraltas tried to run away, some fought back with shovels or picks. Some Peraltas even defended themselves with cast iron pans, concussing their attackers. Yet as much as they tried to resist, all of them were slain that day. Only Miguel, who was working his way up the mountain, was left. The Apache rallied, covered in blood that mixed with their war paint. They circled up and hollered at their victory.

"Today we have won against the people who possess the light!" Alchesay proclaimed among his tribe. "No more will warriors be blinded by their tricks!"

The Apache cheered at their victory. This was of course, deep in Apache territory. The Peraltas were blissfully unaware of how monitored this open land really was.

"Gather what animals you can," Delshay ordered. "Let nothing go to waste." The Apache were quick to gather up the chickens and search through the wreckage. As they broke open crates packed in the wagons, they were shocked to find them filled with rocks. Heavy, yellow rocks scattered the ground and overflowed from every container in camp.

"What is all this?" One of the warriors asked openly. He kicked the gold ore in frustration.

"There's nothing here, move on!" Another ordered. The warriors meandered out of the camp and gathered to begin their march back to their settlement. From behind them, rocks fell down the mountain walls and rolled across the sand into camp. Delshay turned and scanned the ridge, his eyes moved across the cliff faces and needles. Miguel slipped again as he was running to the mine. More rocks broke off beneath his feet and plummeted to the ground below.

Delshay ran through camp and quickly found a trail going up the mountain. He weaved along the switchbacks and climbed over boulders and cliffsides. When he reached the top of the mountain, he saw Miguel disappear into the mine. Delshay flew across the mountain top to catch him. He stopped when he reached the mouth of the mine. The warm light of day seemed to vanish into the black hole in the earth. The young warrior stood daunted and wondered it was worth it to venture in. He turned and saw several other warriors climbing up the mountain. Delshay couldn't be seen standing down in fear. He gripped his axe and lunged into the darkness.

There seemed to be nothing in existence except cold and dark. As his eyes were trying to adjust to the dark, Miguel swung from the shadows and struck Delshay with his fists. He was knocked to the ground and hit his back on a rock protruding from the earth. Delshay yelled in pain and swiped his hand in the darkness in front of him. He caught Miguel's ankle and pulled it out from under him. Miguel fell back into the wall of the mine, his head whipping back against the rock. With his vision going black for a few seconds, Miguel threw down his hands to strike where his enemy was laying. He screamed when he punched solid rock. From behind, Delshay grabbed him and began to choke him with his arm.

Miguel stood up and ran backward, ramming Delshay into the wall. The Apache let go as Miguel tripped. The two men rolled backward, going further into the cave. Both bruising themselves as they tumbled over rocks and lose ore. Yelling came from the mouth of the mine as the other warriors were drawing near. Their vision was stripped from them as they entered the dark. Only one of the Apache walked confidently into that mine. Miguel caught a large rock and picked it up as he jumped to his feet. He heard the native Indian groan in pain where he lay. Miguel took the rock and raised it above his head to smash downward. As he moved to strike, an arrow shot through the darkness and struck Miguel in the chest. He peered into the shadow to see an Apache archer step forward with his eyes painted over. Alchesay. The stone fell out of Miguel's hand as he dropped to his knees and began to cough up blood. Delshay crawled toward his father as they both watched the man breath his last and die.

"Bury the dead," Alchesay turned to the other warriors who made their way into the mine. "Just leave this one," He turned to help his son to his feet then left that dark old mine.

~

Jose woke up with burns over his exposed face. His chapped lips opened, gasping for moisture. His sombrero fell off his head as he stumbled to his feet. He struggled to walk forward, let alone remain upright. Water shimmered a few yards in front of him. He took staggered strides over to the pool then collapsed to meet it. His hands dove into the ground, scooping up only sand. He looked around him. In the distance, more water showed itself. Jose got up again and ran through the sand. But the more he ran toward it, the further the mirage became.

He turned in circles to get a feel for his surroundings. No buildings in sight, no donkey, no nothing. On the horizon was a bump of faraway stones. He squinted with his headache to see the distant peaks of the mountain his camp was in. He took off running toward them. He got a few hundred feet before he fell again. Sand was sticking to his forearms now, both cut and bleeding. He got up and waited for the vertigo to pass before walking yet again toward the mountain.

Out of the mirage on the horizon, came figures marching toward Jose. Figures on horses, figures marching with weapons in their hands. Jose knew there was nowhere to run, so he kept on as the band of Apache approached. They said nothing as they walked past him. Jose stopped and was horrified by the warriors' appearances. They were covered in blood and cuts of their own. They left the boy as they marched back to their land, sparring just the one. Jose turned back to the mountain after they had all passed and ran. After a long while of running, he reached his camp. The tents were cut up, wagon wheels were sticking out of the ground; everything but the three wooden shacks were annihilated.

The boy didn't have enough water in him to cry that day. He only wept with his voice before falling out of consciousness again.

Battle of Picacho Peak, 1862

They say there's two kinds of fast. There's the quick, the light-footed. Swift as a horse running free across the plains. Quick like a gunman's draw or a flash of lightning across the sky. The kind of speed that makes you wonder if'n you even saw it.

Then there's the kind of fast that Lieutenant James Barrett rode with. All rage and haste. The hooves of his horse hit the earth a little harder, cut the dirt a little deeper. His horse snorted and snarled with fire. The kind of fast that a man rides with when he takes matters into his own hands. The kind of speed men charge with into battle.

Lieutenant Barrett and his thirteen rode along the Butterfield Overland Stagecoach line, which had been abandoned since the beginnings of the war. They had done their routine sweep of Picacho Peak, waiting for reinforcements from California's 1st Calvary, when they spotted a Confederate dispatch of their own. These rebels were about fifty miles from their station in Tucson, where just earlier that year, they had driven out or jailed any Union supporters. This band of Confederates had ridden out of their fort to meet recruits rumored to be joining their forces from California. The arrival of the Union's 1st Calvary was supposed to let them know that no such help would come. And that they would drive their rebel cause all the way back to the Atlantic. Only now, Barrett had it in mind to deliver the message himself.

In his blue coat and black cowboy hat, he led the charge of horsemen around the mountain and into the thicket. Towering green saguaro cacti and tangles of bur sage filled the valley low. Boulders dotted the ground, making it even more difficult to traverse on horseback. He held unto his horse with his knees as he pulled out his rifle. His white gloves held onto his gun, raised to his shoulder, and taking aim.

"Go to hell, ye rebels!" Barrett hollered as they thrashed through the wilderness. .58 caliber muskets and carbine repeaters fired through the cacti at the unsuspecting rebels. Their horses jumped at the gunshots; the jolt of fear went up through the Confederate riders as well.

"Bastards!" The rebels returned fire at the approaching enemy. They whipped their mounts and ran to evade. Gunsmoke rose with the sand being kicked up by the riding horses. The thorny brush cutting at the horse's legs as they ran.

"Cover me, I can't reload!" One soldier yelled. His hands fumbled to slide more bullets into the chamber as his horse squealed and bucked in pain. A bullet flew and struck him in the shoulder, sending him off his horse. His grey coat now ripped and soaking up blood. He screamed for his arm, not noticing he had fallen into a bush of prickly pear. As he struggled to get up, needles punctured his uniform and driving into his neck.

Most other soldiers were on their feet, hiding behind boulders for cover. Barrett looked around for the enemies, but in the dense thicket, they were hard to spot. He thought about moving out towards the clearing, but before he could move, a rebel went out from his cover and fired at the lieutenant. The rebel's gun jammed. Barrett took aim but stopped when he dropped his gun and surrendered, his face shaken with horror. Barrett quickly ran over to him and tied his hands behind his back and left him to keep fighting.

Lt. Barrett crept forward toward a rockslide, where one rebel had found vantage to shoot from. The Confederate leaned against the rock, using it to steady his aim. He fired onto a Union soldier who was running between covers. The bullet lodged into the side of his ribs and dropped the young man instantly. Barrett kept low as he circled to the side of the rock pile. He readied his gun with bayonet, breathing short choppy breathes. Then he charged up the rockslide, the ground wabbling beneath his steps. Before the rebel could turn and fire, Barrett's bayonet was stuck through his collarbone. He screamed as blood gushed out from his neck. The rebel covered his wounds with his hands as Barrett left him rolling on the ground.

"Mount up!" Barrett called, seeing two other prisoners tied up with the one who surrendered to him. He saw no other Confederates and all the firing had stopped. The skirmish lasted no more than a few minutes. Most shots were lost between the tangle of thorns. Barrett grabbed one of the prisoners and got atop his horse.

"What'd'ya say boys? We took it to those filthy men, huh? Damn em all!" He laughed and sneered at the prisoners.

A gunshot rang out over his words. Barrett's men looked around in the brush to see who fired or where it struck, but when they looked back, they saw their lieutenant on the ground with a bullet hole through his neck. His lips twitched, trying to breath, but within moments, he was dead.

"Barrett's down!" Echoed over the desert.

"Retreat!" Rob Hickock yelled, one of Barrett's men. The silence was filled again with men mounting their horses and scrambling to get away. The Union soldiers put the prisoners on their horses, sitting backwards behind the saddle. Then the survivors rode off. They looked back as bullets started to fly past them.

"Christ!" The prisoners waved their bound hands, trying to get their comrades to stop shooting.

Eventually, they rode out of range; north from Picacho Peak into more open desert. And as they distanced themselves from one mountain, another came into view. It was dusty, the mirage from the hot air made it red against the yellow sands. Its ridgeline was cut and jagged. At the base of this mountain were a few wooden structures among a field of cacti.

"We take shelter there for the night," One of the Union soldiers pointed to the shacks. The three of them were patchwork. Old boards spaced out enough to call themselves walls. The ceilings were worse. Mere framework with canvas cloth to keep out the sun. The floors were the most secure, still covered in sand, but put together enough to keep the rattlers out.

As the ten remaining riders slowly approached the buildings, they noticed mounds of rock scattered about. Low mounds of loose rock, ovular in shape. Bones of various kinds were also spread over the earth. Some nestling under plants, others stuck into the open sand. They stopped when they spotted atop a lone rock, a skull. The bleach white bone faced them and hiding under its teeth lived a scorpion.

"We should move on," One of the prisoners squirmed at the sight. "We shouldn't be here." His voice echoed against the mountain base.

"Suppose you're looking for a nice bed and breakfast on a quiet ranch?" One of the Union boys snickered.

"Want me to take you back to your friends in Tucson?" Hickock asked.

"Listen here, you damn Yankee! This is Apache ground. Why'd you think there's bones all over the place? Oh, they's probably watching us right now," He turned and scanned the ridgeline. "Figuring out how they's gonna kill us. And *eat* us!"

"Apache don't eat people, you'll be fine," Hickock dismounted his horse and pulled the prisoner onto the ground, unable to catch himself with his hands tied up. He pushed himself to a seated position and spit out the sand he'd just swallowed.

"Fine. Don't believe me. But if we all find ourselves at the other end of Geronimo's gun, don't say I didn't warn ya. This here is Crooked Top Mountain; Apache killed a whole town here once."

"Shut up," Hickock pulled the prisoner to his feet by tie around his wrists, ignoring their raving. The other soldiers were already on the ground, the three prisoners being herded to their own shack. "Tie em up to the posts," he ordered. He was tall and lanky, big bushy beard and balding hair under his Union cap.

"You're leaving us outside?" Another prisoner looked around, noticing the setting sun.

"That way *Geronimo* gets you first," Hickock grinned.

"Him or the rattlesnakes," Another laughed. He was gathering dead wood and brush from the ground, shaking off the sand, and piling them up near the center of camp.

The Union soldiers sat around the fire that night. Their horses were tied up near the shacks. The flame cracked and blazed against the black sky. Stars shone behind the silhouettes of cacti and the mountain.

"We need to let them go," one said.

"What?" Hickock looked over his shoulder to the prisoners. "Why'd you reckon?"

"If we have prisoners, the California Column will know we attacked against orders."

"We tell them they attacked us."

"And when the prisoners tell them a different story?"

"Johnson's right," Another added. "We need to let them go in the morrow and then meet up with the unit. Tell them to head to Tucson as the next initiative."

"What do we say about Barrett?" Hickock asked.

"We've been stationed in the middle of a desert; they won't look twice about having some casualties," Johnson said. He had a thick mustache and long hair combed back behind his ears. He was reclined on the ground, polishing his gun.

Overhead, the stars were slowly covered. The night, growing evermore dark as clouds moved over the camp. A hiss of steam came from the fire between the men. A water droplet splashed off Johnson's gun. A minute later, another hit Rob Hickock on the cheek. Slowly, raindrops started to fall on the men.

"Let's get inside," One of them stood and walked over to the shacks. The others eventually followed, all still dumbfounded at seeing their first rain since they've been stationed in the New Mexico Territory.

"Put the prisoners in their own cabin. Rest of us will split between the two," Johnson went over to untie one of them from their post. He escorted the rebel to his shack, where the other prisoners now were.

"Thank you," The prisoner said as he was led indoors, grateful to be out of the elements. Johnson left and shut the door without a word.

The rain was steadily coming down now, making the desert night all the colder. It drizzled through the ceilings and came through the porous walls. Soldiers on all sides huddled to stay warm and dry, sitting away from the leaks in the roof. Both shacks intended to keep watch, but all men were too tired from the battle to stay awake any longer. They slept soundly in their uniforms. The same set of clothes they lived in, fought in, and would likely die in. Blood and dirt were now washing out of the wool, soaking up the rain. They kept their boots on, too. Far worse was to expose their feet to the cold than to indulge a minor comfort. Besides, everyone who's camped out in the desert knows an open boot will just become shelter for a tarantula or worse. They shivered and waited in their sleep for the rain to stop. Some of them silently tending to their wounds. Despite fighting one of their first battles in the war, all of these men had slept in worse conditions.

~

Sunlight peered through the boards of the shacks the next morning. A crow called down from the cactus it stood on. Rob Hickock was leaning against the outside wall, smoking his morning cigarette. He'd never smoked before the war, but he picked up the habit from his comrades. He wiped his face before taking in another huff. Across the field, one of the prisoners opened the door of his shack. With tied hands, he pulled down his trousers and began to piss onto a shrub nearby. Hickock scoffed at the sight, then flicked away his cigarette and went back inside.

"You told the prisoners we're letting them go?" One soldier asked. Hickock shook his head.

"Not yet. Figured we'd keep em long as possible. Maybe have em brush off the horses."

"We have an extra, you know? Horse."

"Huh?"

"Well, if we're letting em go anyway. Might as well give em a horse. They'd die out here otherwise."

"Sure, let's just hold their hands as we walk them back to Tucson. Let them fight against us one more time," He scoffed. "Never."

"So, what was your plan?"

"Keep them tied up and ride off."

"They'd die."

"Not my problem," Hickock grabbed his rifle from the floor and slung it over his shoulder. He turned to head back outside.

"Cut their ties, Rob," The other soldier said as the door closed on him.

By now, most were already awake. Soldiers were wringing out their coats and picking on what little food they had packed with em. Rob Hickock walked over to the three prisoners who sat in the shade of the porch.

"Surprised you didn't run off," he said.

"Hundreds of miles of open desert. Be futile," One of them replied.

"Wise," he said through his long beard. "Cause we're gonna cut you a deal."

"Alright. We're listening," another said.

"We can't bring you three with us when we ride out today to meet back up with our company. So, we're letting you go."

"In exchange for what?"

"For not turning back around when you meet up with your company."

"How do you know we won't?"

"Ya'll could've ran last night but you didn't. Suppose we gotta trust you."

"Trust? In the middle of a war that's split families in two," He chuckled. "I don't know how much trust there is to go round."

"You giving me a reason not to trust you?" Hickock took his rifle off his shoulder. "Huh?"

"Just busting your chops, Yankee," The prisoner said.

From across camp Johnson yelled over.

"Hickock, we're saddling up, let's go!"

"Yeah, alright," Rob waved him off. He took out his knife and cut the rope that bound their wrists. "Told we're giving you one of our horses. So, I guess pick which one of you makes it out of here," With that, Rob got up and walked over to his horse.

"Wait..." Owen said to the other prisoners as they were getting up. He had short black hair and a roughly shaven face. As the Union soldiers were preoccupied that morning preparing their horses and talking to one another, they failed to notice something had changed overnight. The graves of rock were washed clean by the rain and shone in the sunlight.

"What is it?" Claude asked. He was tallest of the three, but not the brightest. Balding and not a hair on his chin, Claude somehow looked both old and young. "Is it Indians?" He looked around frightfully.

"Don'tcha see it?" Owen said quietly. "On the ground."

"What?"

"All over the graves. Gold."

"Shit," Hiram, the third prisoner, laughed with his gut.

"Shh! I don't think they know and if we're smart, it'll stay that way," Owen cautioned.

"Does this mean we're rich?" Claude's eyes widened.

"Soon," He nodded. "Hiram, you take the horse to Tucson. Tell them the Northerners know we're held up there and then tell em to send some workers this way. If there's gold lying about the graves, that means there's a mine nearby."

"What about us?" Claude asked.

"We're going to stay and gather up as much as we can. We're going to start a little town here. And the first thing's the bank."

"What about the war, Owen?" Hiram asked.

"You can go die for your salary. Hell, take mine. With what I can see from here, we're gonna be much richer if we stay."

"What about the Apache?" Claude stood up and looked around. "Now that the Yankees are gone, we're defenseless."

"Quit your crying. There's probably some old tools buried around here," Owen said.

"Tools?" asked Hiram.

"Either way, I think we'll be just fine. Besides, the closest Indians are probably the Pinal, the ones we traded with a while back." Owen shrugged.

"Right," Hiram scoffed. "You boys gather up that ore. I'll be back with some workers. Tell em we found a whole field of gold. Hope you know what you're doing, Owen."

"My father was a city planner back east. I know what we'll need," Owen assured. Hiram shook his head and kicked his horse to ride.

Battle of Apache Pass, 1862

Hiram rode the pale brown horse swiftly south toward Tucson. Its hooves chopped up the dirt of the open flatland. Don't let the name fool you. Out there, it was anything but flat terrain. The world is rougher than sandpaper. Gulches and gullies dig through the hard ground. Boulder stacks pepper the earth between the tall saguaros. As fast as he could safely ride, Hiram navigated the wilderness to deliver the mixed news. He was stout and had a bushy black beard with equally large eyebrows. His hair was short, combed back under his confederate cap.

Now Tucson was the biggest town within a few hundred miles. Suppose it served as an oasis to the expansive deserts of the New Mexico Territory. It was sizeable for being out in the desert, being around since before the Mexican War. It had all the commodities of civilized life: stores, schoolhouses, and a fair number of farms. Many coach roads and trails going westward went through this city. Meaning, most prospectors travelled through these parts during the California rush. And would return on their way back east. It was walled with adobe most-way around the city with tall arches at each entrance. The Confederates built up the defenses when they occupied the city. They added watch towers and artillery around the perimeter. As far as the West was concerned, this was the prized stronghold.

Hiram rode over the hill to reach the final stretch of trail. He nearly jumped out of his skin when he saw thousands of soldiers in blue. Whole divisions of calvary, foot soldiers, and artillery all marching down the road. Wagons with horses and mules, all packed with supplies and munitions. The Union.

"Shit," He rubbed his forehead. Hiram felt his grey cap and realized he was still in uniform. He quickly threw off his hat and unbuttoned his coat. He'd have to make do with grey pants, white tee shirt, and suspenders. Some of the solders walking by saw him but didn't change their cadence. Hiram kicked his horse and whipped the reins, passing the California Column.

"Watch it, would'ya?" One of the officers hollered as Hiram veered past them. His horse cutting them off. One of the soldiers ran up and knelt on the ground, drawing a bead on the fleeing rider. "Leave him. There's not much they can do now."

Hiram passed under the adobe gate and rode along the wooden store faces. Most buildings shared walls and porches. Buildings like the saloon and the jail stood on their own, built with adobe and brick. No one paid Hiram any mind when ran through; horses sprinted in and out of this town so often with the war. Though this would be the last message to be received here.

Fittingly, the rebels were held up in the old mail station. Cots were sprawled along the open floor. Old horse pens were made into offices or private quarters for the officers. A telegram station clicked in the middle of the room with operators writing down incoming messages and tapping the switch to send messages of their own. A fairly new invention, considering electricity itself was rare this far west.

"The Column's here!" Hiram yelled over the milling soldiers. Officers looked up from their papers, men sat up in their cots.

"Good. We've been in desperate need of some reinforcements," Captain Hunter nodded then went back to his clipboard. "Governor Baylor must've approved our request. Get-"

"We ain't getting no reinforcements," Hiram went further into the building. All eyes were turned to him now. "A few thousand Union boys are marching on us right now. Guns, calvary, everything."

"A few *thousand*?" Hunter whispered.

"That's right. Saw em with my own eyes," Hiram nodded. "Whatever defenses we think we have here, it won't be enough for the guns they're packing."

"We estimated their numbers to be in the hundreds. If'n that's true, then we're gravely outnumbered. And more so than we once thought," the officer walked over to him.

"You knew they were coming?" Hiram asked.

"That's right. We've been finding supply caches that the sympathizers have been placing for them. We estimated a few hundred based on what we gathered. We destroyed their resources of course, but we didn't think they would have over eight hundred. Which, if you noticed, would *still* have outnumbered us."

A couple of soldiers came running into the station. Their hats were crooked on their sweating hair. Out of breath, the young soldier pointed backwards, out the door.

"Yankees. Bout two thousand," The scout said. "Just over the ridge."

"Jesus Christ," Hunter said. Murmuring broke out over the hundred or less. The captain, older and bearded, looked around in the panic of his men. "Get your things!" He ordered. "Company A, moving out!"

"Pack up, we're moving out," Another officer of the Arizona Rangers repeated. The soldiers stationed there scrambled to pack their bags, tearing down the kitchen and telegram station.

"Get those papers packed away, we leave nothing for the yanks. Got it?" Captain Hunter ordered.

"Yes sir."

After the war broke out, the confederates declared this land a part of their "Arizona Territory." Not wanting to recognize themselves as part of the Union's "New Mexico." The self-proclaimed governor, Mr. Baylor, organized a detachment to replace the existing militia here. Taking after the boys in Texas, the Arizona Rangers were founded to be elite fighting force of the West. Seventy-five of the finest cavalrymen would make up this company, roaming the lawless territory and keeping order (As much as a rebel company can keep). Most importantly, they would be taking the fight to any Union soldier or supporter they found.

But now wasn't the time for fighting. From the sounds of it, the boys from California had more horsemen than Hunter's entire force. No, this was the time to run. They all knew they were outnumbered and out matched. Even if Tucson had all the defenses in place, there was no war they would make this city into a battleground. They packed up, loaded their supplies onto wagons and horses and left with only a handful of soldiers behind.

"You boys sure you want to stay back?" Captain Hunter asked Hiram from atop his horse. The entire force was out in the street, getting their own horses ready for departure.

"Yes sir. We'll keep watch and won't fire no guns. In case the Column doesn't end up occupying the town, we'll send word," Hiram replied.

"Very well, soldier," Hunter nudged his horse to start walking, catching up with the parade of Confederates leaving east out of the city. The soldiers who hung back walked over to Hiram after the last of the Rangers disappeared beyond the town walls.

"You sure about this?"

"Yes, I'm sure. We'll be fine. Maybe ditch your coats so we don't get thrown into some Northern prison," he said to the crew.

"We're not worried about them, Hiram. We want to make sure that there's gold before we trek across the open desert," one said, sinching down his saddle.

"Now why would I lie about a thing like that? There's gold. Them mountains are probably rich with veins. But if you don't want a piece, then you can pass it off to the next settler. Cause, I'll tell you what, people are going to come and they're going to buy up plots of our land. We might just serve them gold nuggets we found for free out of the saloon."

"Alright, quit your tall tales. You found something out there, but we'll see for ourselves just how much."

"You won't regret it," Hiram smiled through his thick beard. "You see Owen when you get there. I'm sure he can set you up with a place to pitch your tent. Hell, if you pray on the ride there, he may give you a job. Tell people where you're heading too. A town only works if we get enough people to do all the jobs."

The soldiers spent the night in Tucson and began telling everyone the news Hiram delivered. Gold had been found south of the Salt River. Near that lonesome, jagged mountain. The saloons stirred that night with anticipation. Maybe for once they would get lucky. Stories of the gold grew and changed as it passed from ear to ear. Some were skeptical, most had high hopes, but no one would even come close to knowing all what would happen.

~

Early the next morning, covered wagons were loaded up with lumber and barrels of supplies. Men packed their mules full of equipment. Each man, or family carried their own provisions, their own mementos from life back in the East. Each family having their own story, their own culture. But on each hip or across each back, was a gun. That was always the same.

Hiram remained in town to buy supplies for his crew. First, he found a wagon that seemed unoccupied and—after looking both ways—hitched his horse to it. He went to the gold refinery and took out the nuggets he packed with him. The clerks weighed the raw ore and paid out cash at the standard rate of $16 an ounce. Then Hiram bought crates of food out of the general store and three six-shooters with boxes of ammo. After buying himself a new hat, he was ready to set out for the field of gold.

A few miles from town, the parade of prospectors passed an army marching down the road. The two groups exchanged looks, but both were too determined to stop. Colonel James Carleton rode on into Tucson, slowly looking around at the emptying streets. Behind the captain of the Column flew a flag of red and white stripes. A blue block was in the top corner with stars that surrounded an eagle. In its talons was a ribbon that read, *E Pluribus Unum*. "Out of many, One." The heavy flag waved softly behind Carleton in the still winds. What the soldiers saw as a symbol of unity and freedom, many people saw as oppression. Freedom to them was states' rights. Freedom to the Northerners was liberty for slaves. These clashing ideals drove a wedge between brother states, creating a divide that I'd wager exists to this day. As Carleton and his men occupied the town, they found it totally abandoned of rebel fighters.

"They're not here," An old lady said, standing on her porch and smoking a cigarette. Her thin grey hair was tied up in a bun.

"Where are they?"

"Who knows?" She spoke. "But you missed them by a day."

"Then we can still catch em," Carleton thought aloud. He wore a blue coat with brass buttons and black trousers with shiny black boots. His hair was brown and parted at the side, with mutton chops growing down the sides of his face and blending into his mustache. "Roberts!" He called behind him, turning his horse around.

"Yes sir?" Captain Thomas Roberts walked his horse over to his commanding officer. He was middle-aged and had short, greying hair. His mustache was curled up slightly at the edges.

"Take your detachment and ride out. See if you can catch em."

"Yes sir."

"Send Cremony and his men with you, huh?"

"Yes sir," Roberts turned and went to John Cremony, the other leading officer in the Column. While the officers gathered their men and guns, Carleton filled the town with the remaining soldiers. People stared out the shade of their windows, into the white sunlight outside.

The town had switched control in the past when this land was ceded by Mexico. Settlers were offered citizenship in the United States if they stayed or granted passage back to their country. When the next war broke out, the Confederates quickly turned the city into a fort, getting rid of anyone who opposed their stance.

Now, the Union was going to repay the rebel sympathizers the same courtesy. They weren't going to sanction anywhere for confederates to live on their own. As much as this war was about states' rights, it was also about keeping the states united. It was seen as controlling by Southerners, but the Union wasn't going to allow a break from their country. So, those soldiers occupied that town, which would remain a part of the union to this day. And the people would have to get on with it or flee with the rest of the Confederates back to Texas.

"March on!" Roberts kicked his horse and marched his men east out of Tucson. Flags of red, white, and blue flew behind them. The same flag now raised on the flagstaff in the center of town. The companies marched along the coach road, following the tracks they knew were left not a day ago. Two dozen calvary were scattered throughout the hundred or so infantrymen walking the hot road. A few artillery pieces were pulled along with them.

They marched forth, under the hot sun. At this point, the Column had only known the war as one long march. They had walked from the California coast to the heart of the New Mexico territory without any action. Their only battle had been against the unforgiving land. This promise of finally seeing the war left the soldiers with mixed emotions. They'd been waiting to take it to the Confederates, but the nerves of walking into your first battle is unparalleled.

"We'll break here," Roberts got off his horse when his unit reached Dragoon Springs. Ruined stone buildings left reminders of life that used to be here. After the mail route was abandoned, stations like this one began to fall into disarray. Old stones stood where arched doorways used to be. Men took turns scooping water from the spring with their tin dishes or ladles. It was warm and dirty, but it was water. So, the soldiers drank it up right along with their horses.

"You think we'll catch em?" Cremony went up to Roberts, who was pouring water over his head. John Cremony was a lean man. He kept himself good and clean despite traveling through the war. He wore pomade in his hair and kept his mustache trimmed. Over his shirt, he wore a poncho to keep the dust off him. The standard officer's coat was too warm for this weather anyway.

"I don't know. We've been marching pretty hard, but I'd doubt we'd catch up unless they stopped somewhere round here."

"Let's hope they stay on the run. We don't want another battle like Glorieta... Hell, everyone died over there."

"If we shoot smart, we don't need to worry about that. From our reports, what we brought with us should be doubled of their forces."

"That might not be enough. Heard the Rangers are damn good fighters," Cremony admitted.

"We caught them on the run, John. If they see us, my guess is they'll keep on running."

"I hope your right, then," Cremony looked at the soldiers who were finding shade and quenching their dire thirst. "Onward, then?"

Roberts nodded. The officers mounted their horses and circled around the stone ruins to muster the infantry again. Despite their groans, they formed ranks and started down the road. The evening sun beat on their backs as they marched in cadence.

The road climbed up, weaving between two shallow peaks. In the distance, the desert was laid out to the ends of the horizon. The kept marching straight into the pass. There were shadows moving in the thickets, and little pebbles jumping down the rocky slopes. Cremony looked around from atop his horse, scanning the ridge lines surrounding them. The sounds of a hundred marching men echoed off the peaks and masked anything else that might make a sound.

A shot rang out over the pass. Sand flew up at the feet of Cremony's horse.

"Dammit!" Cremony grunted.

At first there was nothing. Then, another shot. Shouting rang out from the hills with the sounds of gunfire. The rocks and trees all yelled in chorus.

"Apache!" Roberts took out his rifle. From behind rock walls built in the pass, native fighters alternated between firing on the soldiers below and reloading their rifles. The infantry took out their rifles, returning fire to the hills surrounding them. Bullets flew across the pass and ricocheted off the stones. Cremony rode back and jumped off his horse, taking cover behind a large boulder. The Apache hailed down bullets into the mass of soldiers.

"Formations!" Roberts ordered. The soldiers made lines, half facing their respective hill side. The first row knelt down and fired uphill. The men behind them were reloading the muskets and handing them back to the front fighters.

Behind one of the stone walls, Delshay quickly reloaded his gun and turned to fire, hitting a soldier in the arm. In the years after his father died, he had traveled south with this band of Apache, helping gain back their land from the flood of incoming settlers. He never rode with Geronimo, but this band of fighters were a spark off of his flame nonetheless. He turned and fired another shot, the bullet ringing out as it ricocheted off the stone ground. He wore red markings on his face and biceps, much the same as the other Apache.

"We can't see em!" One soldier yelled. They only saw puffs of smoke rising behind hiding places. Gun barrels just barely stuck out from the rocks, making it almost impossible to see where the enemy was or how numerous they were. Cremony saw the confusion below and jumped into action.

"Calvary, uphill!" Cremony got back on his horse and drew his sword. Riders followed the charge up the sides of the hills and fired down onto the exposed attackers. Apache near the bottom of the hill turned their fire to the charging horses. They fired on the calvary with six-shooters. Some even dared their knives or axes, jumping onto the riders and throwing them off their horses.

Atop the hill an old Apache stood wearing a red shirt and leather vest. His black hair fell past his shoulders. He fired down on the horses. Striking one, it fell and sent the rider tumbling down the rocks. Cremony stopped and looked down on the chaos of his soldiers. Bullets flew in every direction, some whizzing past dangerously close to him.

"We need to get out of here!" He turned his horse around and rode down the hill. "Roberts!" The other officer saw his comrade and followed suit.

"Retreat!" Roberts ordered. "Retreat!" The units ran back toward the mouth of the pass and hid themselves around the corner and out of harm's way. Only a few bodies remained, bleeding into the dusty ground. Men were sitting behind boulders, collecting themselves. They slowly reloaded their guns and took their time to mend their wounds when they realized they weren't being pursued. The pass glowed red in the setting sun. The desert ignites with fiery color at sunup or sundown. Reds and yellows are drawn out from the tan, pale desert of noonday. Shadows of deep purple are cast by cactus of emerald and needles of golden rock.

Cremony looked up, catching his breath in the peacefulness of the moment. He saw the two Howitzer guns, still sitting where they were when the soldiers were first attacked. Sending the quiet scene back into chaos, he cleared his throat and got the attention of the operators. Then he tilted his head toward the pass. The men loaded the cannons and aimed each of them at a peak, then fired. The explosions shattered the silence. Dirt flew high into the air with each impact. Screams came from inside the pass.

"Again," He ordered quietly. The guns were reloaded and pushed back into position. They fired again, both peaks blowing up again.

"Infantry, get ready!" Roberts called out. Men formed a line, blocking the mouth of the pass, in case fighters came funneling from around the corner.

"Again." The Howitzers thundered and sent fire and dirt into the air. "Again." From around the bend, one Apache came running. Lines of soldiers took aim. His hands waved in the air, no weapon on him.

"Hold," Roberts said. The Apache yelled words not known to the Union soldiers. But they understood the point. They surrendered. The Union soldiers backed down and watched the Apache continue to approach. The Apache pointed at Cremony and waved for him to follow. Without hesitation, John Cremony stepped forward.

"What are you doing?" Roberts asked.

"They might want to meet with an officer. Discuss terms of surrender."

"And if they shoot you?"

Cremony mouthed "Again," as he walked away. He was led around the bend and up on of the hills to a tent that had been pitched. A few campfires dotted the slopes of the pass, as Apache kept warm and kept watch. He followed the man up and over the peak and down into a tent. There, Cremony was met by the Apache with the red shirt and leather vest. He was laying down with blankets covering him. Cremony sat down next to him.

"*Dagot'ee*," The Apache greeted, raising his hand only a few inches of his chest.

"D-" Cremony looked around in confusion. "*Dagot'ee?* Hello?"

"Hello..." The Apache repeated. He pointed to himself. "Mangas Colorado," He was struggling to find the strength to speak. Then Mangas pointed at Cremony.

"John. John Cremony," He caught on.

"*Yiyaa*," Mangas pointed to his eye. Then he pointed at Cremony's rifle.

"Gun," he said.

"Gun..." Mangas repeated. Then he opened his vest to show a bullet hole through the sternum. "Gun."

"Jesus," Cremony muttered.

"Gun stop."

"Yeah, the guns will stop," Cremony nodded. Mangas nodded along with him.

"John Cremony," Mangas reached out and squeezed John's arm before letting him go.

~

In the morning, the soldiers passed through. The dirt was stained red, where men had bled out on the slopes. Apache bodies were bent over fortifications and buried with the rockslides caused by the cannon fire. The soldiers walked quietly through the peaks, in awe at the destruction of their Howitzer guns. About seventy bodies total were left in the cold earth that day.

Atop the hill, Delshay was trying to steady his breath, sitting on the ground with a broken foot. He hadn't slept that night, too busy in pain to relax. Shards of a bomb had lodged themselves in his lower shin and into the top of his foot. He needed to remove the shrapnel, or he'd lose the limb.

"Medicine man," He grunted for help as he tried to stand. He collapsed back to his seat. He yelled out in pain. "Get me the medicine man," he said in his own language.

"Can't you see? He's busy," One of the Apache said, also going around to find the wounded.

"I need to fix my leg," he said. The other looked at the torn and swollen foot.

"You'll slow us down."

"What?"

"We have to leave you," he said as he moved down the slope to gather with the survivors.

"I need help!" Delshay yelled.

"You want help? Drag yourself to Tucson. There's a white medic there. He'll help you," With that, he left Delshay on the ground to muster with the other Apache. They were still a few hundred strong and greatly outnumbered the Northerners but couldn't withstand another bombardment from the artillery.

Looking down the hill, Delshay saw a few ponies standing behind the tents. He began to scoot down, sliding on the rocks, and keeping his right foot extended in front of him. Soon, he reached the bottom of the hill. He looked around for anyone who might spot him. No one. He grabbed the horn of the horse's saddle and pulled himself up. Keeping his head low, he kicked the horse to slowly walk forward.

"Hey!" A shout came from behind him. He turned to see the Apache who left him. Delshay whipped the horse and got it to running speed. They turned around the bend of the pass and down the hill back toward Tucson.

Boom Town, 1863

Delshay rode into Tucson. His foot was seeping with blood and leaving a trail in the street. He threw his hands up when several men took out their rifles and aimed at the Apache. Pointing to his foot, he yelled for a doctor in his own tongue. The men on the road looked at each other. One of them walked around to see what he was pointing at.

"Judas priest!" The man gasped. "A doctor? You need a doctor?"

"Doctor," Delshay nodded, tears running from his eyes.

"Where's the doctor?" He turned and asked the bystanders.

"Army doctors all left, probably in Texas already but the Northerners may have a surgeon with em," Someone answered.

"I ain't going to no Yankee doctor," The man turned and spat.

"It ain't your life, Bill. Take him in!"

"No! I hate them more than I hate these Apache," He snapped. "What happened to the town surgeon?"

"He's left for the boom town," said an old woman who sat on her porch, smoking a cigarette. "Surprised anyone's left here."

"Can you still ride?" Bill asked Delshay, laying his hand on the horse. The Apache grimaced and nodded. "Alright, follow me."

Bill walked across the street and jumped onto his horse. He whipped and took off down the road. Delshay kicked and ran to follow. A few miles out of town, they veered off the mail route and followed the impression left in the dirt, heading north. They rode along the banks of a dried-up river. They rode past Picacho Peak and into the flatlands. On the horizon was a jagged rock mass.

"Yeah, that's the one. The Crooked Top," Bill pointed to the mountain. "Looks like a razorback hog, or that's what they said. The town they're building should be just at the base." He whipped his horse to continue. Delshay followed behind and realized where he was going, recognizing that distinct ridgeline. He'd been here before.

The town was already filling out and taking shape. Buildings were being built in rows; tents pitched between them. Owen had marked out plots and sold them for a hundred bucks a piece. He had bought some lumber from incoming settlers and patched up one of the shacks, making a bank. He and Claude gathered all the gold nuggets they could find and stored them in barrels inside the bank. Hiram had even bought a safe when he was in Tucson. That kept all the cash they were getting from plot sales. A few thousand dollars on the first day wasn't bad for the three rebels.

The surgeon pitched his tent near the center of town. It was large and held several beds with tables full of tools and open bottles of elixir. Bill opened the tent flap and helped Delshay limp to the nearest bed.

"What happened?" Doctor Thorne asked. He was tall, grey hair and a bloody stained coat. Round glasses hung on his nose.

"Don't know, he just showed up in town like this."

"Here?" The doctor put on a thick apron.

"No, Tucson."

"You boys rode from Tucson?"

"Yeah, heard you left to come here."

"That I did... Now, let's take a look," Doctor Thorne moved the bloody foot, looking at the pieces stuck into it. Delshay cringed in pain. The doctor dropped his foot and moved to his medicine cabinet. He took a glass bottle of dark liquid and handed it to the Apache.

"Drink," He ordered. Delshay popped off the cork and sniffed the contents. His eyebrows perked up a little bit, then he took a swig and set the bottle on the ground. The doctor took it and splashed some on the foot. Delshay let out a yell of pain. Then he took leather straps and tied his foot down to the bed.

"Find him something to bite down on," Doctor Thorne waved at Bill. He was in his twenties, but he looked the part of a full man. He wore simple suspenders over his loose button-up shirt covered by a long duster coat and a wide hat. He had a thick black beard and sharp eyes.

Bill looked around and found a spare tent stake, then handed it off to the Apache. Delshay bit down on the iron stake and nodded for the doctor to continue. Thorne splashed some more alcohol onto the cut-up foot. Delshay shook and grunted with the sting. Then, Thorne took out large tweezers and forceps. He pinched onto one piece of shrapnel, then opened the wound slightly to pull out the full piece of steel. Delshay laid his head back, trying to breath. He began to sweat and became lightheaded.

"Get him some water. In the box, there," Doctor Thorne gestured with his bloodied hands. Bill got up from the cot he was sitting on and went to the open crate of glass bottles of water. "Put some on a cloth and cool him off, dab his mouth, too."

"Yes, sir," Bill sighed. He did what he asked, getting a cloth wet and patting the Apache's forehead and mouth. Doctor Thorne started on another larger piece of steel. He could pull it only a quarter inch before it became stuck. Delshay screamed as he bit down on the tent stake.

"What's going on?" Bill looked around.

"It's caught between the bones," The doctor said calmly. "Pinched between the first and second metatarsals. Give him another shot of whiskey, this is going to hurt."

Bill rushed to the bottle and poured a little swig into Delshay's mouth. The Apache looked around in terror.

"Hold this piece, with the tweezers. I need two hands for this. And don't move it until I say so," Thorne handed off the tool to Bill. Using the forceps, Doctor Thorne pushed into the foot, then opened the forceps to widen the space between the bones.

"Now," he said. Bill pulled straight up. Doctor Thorne quickly closed and removed the forceps. Delshay was biting down in fury, crying, and shaking his head.

"Just a few more pieces. Then we'll have to stitch you together."

After the doctor had finished up, Delshay sat up in the bed. Bill had wandered off to find the town saloon.

"Do you have money?" Thorne asked. The Apache stared blankly at him. Thorne washed his hands, took out his wallet, then pulled out a few dollar bills. "Money?" Delshay shook his head slowly. An object on the doctor's desk caught his eye.

It shimmered and glowed a bit. The Apache pointed to it. Doctor Thorne turned around and picked it up. He held the tiny piece of gold between them.

"I found *this* when I was setting up shop. Supposedly, others have been finding em all around here."

"Money," Delshay pointed at it.

"Yeah, this is money," He nodded.

"More."

"You can bring me more?" Thorne waved his finger between them. Delshay nodded.

"Follow me."

Delshay walked the doctor out of town that night. The Apache had packed a light satchel and a dagger. He was limping still, but he could walk. Campfires shone against the open black skies, casting shadows on the towering mountain walls. Sparks danced with the stars that marched across the night. Tents were spread out around the town's center. Unfished structures looked like wooden skeletons, their ribs hollow and exposed to the desert elements. Few people were up and those who were, were a few drinks passed sober.

The two walked out of the town, toward the base of the mountain. Delshay gave the doctor a strip of fabric.

"What's this?" Thorne asked. Delshay covered his eyes with his hand then pointed at the doctor. Thorne grumbled, took it, and tied it around his eyes. The Apache then led the doctor up the graded mountain side. They twisted around the invisible trail and scaled short walls of rock. Delshay led the doctor up to the top of the mountain, where he'd gone years earlier. They walked to the mouth of the mine, where Delshay took off the blindfold.

"What is this?" The doctor gasped at the sight of the deep cavern. Delshay lit a lamp he'd brought with. The ground and walls glittered with gold. Loose nuggets were scattered about and veins wrapped all around them.

"Money," said Delshay. He handed the doctor a bag. Thorne took it and immediately began to fill it with gold nuggets and any piece of rock with traces of gold in it. He went up and down the mine, looking for leftover ore to scoop up. As he went down the dark mine, away from the glowing light of the lantern, he saw another material on the ground.

"What the hell?" Doctor Thorne said as he beheld a human skeleton. Slowly, Delshay came behind him. "Are you going to kill me?" The doctor turned and asked, pointing at the skeleton. He clenched the bag of gold in his hands. Delshay was expressionless as he saw the remains. He simply handed the doctor the blindfold. Thorne took it as a sign they were leaving, and that he wouldn't be harmed. After saving his leg, Thorne had good reason to believe that the Apache wouldn't cross him.

La Taberna

One of the first buildings to be completed in the boom town was the tavern, *La Taberna*. It was two stories high and had a large red sign that stood even higher. It was owned by Roberto Perez, a Mexican man who'd managed another saloon back in Tucson. The wooden dark building had a set of double doors in the front that swung openly between the hot, bright streets and the dusky interior. The lights were low over the mahogany counter bar. Men played cards on round tables and flirted with the tavern wenches. Most had drinks and smoked cigars, filling the room with an ambiance of relaxation from the hard labor outside.

Bill had stuck around town, often gambling to make a living. He had a solid brown beard and bright eyes. His shotgun leaned against the leg of the table, out of the way. A wide black hat shadowed his face as he looked at his hand. A king, pair of sevens, a three, and an ace. He looked up to study the eyes of the other players. Some raised eyebrows, a sigh, and one other who held a stone face across the table, the dealer. Bill threw in a few dollars. He didn't have a tremendous hand, but he's seen worse. Another gentleman slid a couple dollars to the center of the table. One shook his head and folded, not wagering anything more on his hand. They flipped over their cards. The dealer had a straight, the other had two pairs.

"Well, looky there," The one man sighed with relief and collected his cash.

"Again," The man with the stone face said, who'd lost with the two pairs.

"Alright, there's no rush to this," The man who won said as he stuffed his coat with last round's winnings. They threw their cards in and the dealer shuffled them again and dealt. The players bought in and the game began. Bill looked at his new hand, then immediately went to study the faces of the other players. The man who won the last round was feeling good again and put in a fair amount of his money back to the center table. The dealer smirked.

Bill saw all of this and looked at his hand again. He had a two, three, four, five, and six all of the same suit, a straight flush. It was a strong hand for sure, but would it be enough? The dealer seemed confident. Bill scratched his beard and threw in a few dollars; it was a safe bet. The stone-faced man looked up at Bill. The man who folded last game threw down his cards again and left the table. Cards were turned over. The winner of last game had a pair of jacks. The dealer turned over his cards to show four aces. Bill blinked with disbelief.

"Wait a minute," The man who left came back.

"You're out of the game," The dealer said coldly and reached for his pistol. The man stopped in his tracks. Bill reached over and flipped over the man's abandoned cards. He also had an ace.

"Five aces don't add up," Bill said. The dealer drew and pointed his pistol across the table. Bill looked down the barrel, then revealed his cards. "Besides, *I* won."

"You cheater! You've been cheating us all day!" The man who won last game stood up and yelled. The tavern silenced.

Seeing the gun, the wenches ran upstairs. The dealer turned and aimed at him. Bill pulled his shotgun and fired at the dealer from under the table. The dealer fell over, his legs peppered with wounds. Screams came the patrons inside. The dealer reached out and fired at Bill, the bullet grazing his arm. A dealer at a different table pulled his gun and drew it on Bill. They were working together! The barrel only inches from the side of his face. Bill posted up with his elbow, the gun firing into the ceiling and through the second floor. Bill then hit the man with the butt of his shotgun. He collapsed onto the ground and Bill fired into his chest.

"¿Qué estás hacienda? ¡Disparaste a mi edificio!" Roberto yelled from behind the counter. "Sal de aquí! Sal de aquí!"

"Shut it," Bill stepped over the dead body. Some young men outside ran into the building to see what had happened. "Someone clean this up. And you," Bill pointed at Roberto as he his winnings from the table. "Your dealers better not be cheating us again."

"Sal de aquí," Roberto pushed him out of the tavern. Bill adjusted his coat as he stepped out into the street. His arm bled into the fabric and began to sting.

"Dammit," Bill looked at the cut. He walked across the dusty street and down a few buildings to the doctor's office. It was a wooden building now with a few beds. A small counter separated the operating room from the lobby where tonics and cures were stocked for sale.

"I heard the shooting, what happened Bill?" Doctor Thorne came from the back when he heard the bell above the door ring.

"Yeah, that was me. Damn card dealers over at the Taberna were cheating us."

"Well, sit down. Were you shot anywhere else?" Thorne led him to the back.

"No, just got grazed here," Bill took off his duster coat and rolled up the sleeve on his white button up. The bullet carved out part of his bicep, leaving a wide gash.

"Hold this to the wound," Thorne handed Bill some gauze. "Will I be expecting any more gunshot victims?" He asked, looking over the brim of his glasses.

"No, they'll need the mortician."

"I see," Thorne brought over a bottle of alcohol and dabbed some onto a washcloth. He cleaned the wound and stitched it up in no more than a half-hour.

"I really appreciate this, Doc," Bill said as he paid with his newly won cash.

"No worries. Rough men like you keep men like me in business," Thorne poured himself a glass of whiskey.

"Ain't that somethin'," Bill chuckled, then put on his hat and coat. "Good day to you, Doc."

"Bill," He nodded in goodbye.

~

Over the months, Bill had made himself known as the man who shot down the crooked dealers. Suppose that made him the first lawman of the town, upholding justice in the gambling rooms. That's how the settlers saw it anyway. Not that Bill ever saw himself wearing the star, he was a fierce rebel. A rebel against his country who'd moved out west to escape the laws and ways of society. But with the Column suppressing the rebellion, it seemed he couldn't run forever.

Even with his tendencies to fight against high society, he seemed to have a knack for justice. Or at least, settling scores.

Bill and his shotgun paid visits to people who'd robbed or wronged anyone in camp. At first, he didn't like that people sought him out to deal with their issues, but when people started to offer cash... he couldn't pass it up.

"Dawson and his boys are held up in Salt River Canyon," A man said quietly.

"How many?" Bill loaded cartridges into his double-barreled shotgun.

"Four, maybe five."

"Five men? Are you kidding me?"

"Look, do you want Dawson gone or not?" The man asked. They were standing outside the Taberna, where men knew to find Bill. "The man's a menace. He's been taking advantage of some of the young women here. There ain't nothing they can do about it. Men would stand up to him if it weren't for his gang."

"Course I want Dawson gone," Bill shook his head and spit on the ground.

"Then you'll have to get through his posse," The man replied.

"I can't take five alone. We need more gun power."

"*We* is right. I'm coming with."

"Just for this job, though. I don't make long term partnerships."

"Understood, but if you need an ally down the road. Well, I'd have your back."

"You survive Salt River Canyon, and we'll see if I want your help ever again," Bill chuckled. They saw a skinny young man walking up the street towards them. Bill nodded in his direction. "Get your brother, too. I hear he's gotten pretty good with a gun."

"Jesse's too young to be out fighting," The man shook his head.

"You want Dawson gone?"

"Dammit, Bill. Don't turn this around on me. I hired you to take him out and I'm offering you my hand. But leave my kid brother out of this."

Jesse walked up the wooden steps to meet them. He had a bright smile on his face, same one he wore most every day.

"Jed. Bill. How ya'll doing?" He spoke.

"Afternoon, Jesse," Bill tipped his hat with a smirk. Jed glared over at him.

"What're you guys talking about?" He was only in his teens, still naïve but full of life. He had the same dirty blonde hair as his brother.

"Just talking about you, actually," Bill replied. "Your big brother and I are fixing up a job. Serving real justice."

"You want my help then?" Jesse's eye grew with excitement.

"No, you gotta stay and take care of ma at the ranch. You can't be playing with guns," Jed turned him down. In all ways, Jedidiah Thatcher was a bigger man than his kid brother. He was taller and built like a bull. His face was filled out with a healthy goatee, unlike Jesse who just started to grow facial hair.

"The boy's old enough. I'd say he can make his own decisions," Bill said.

"No," Jed was stern.

"Oh, c'mon Jed. You ain't pa," said Jesse.

"No, I ain't," He snapped. "But he would've wanted me to keep you alive."

"You heard Bill, I'm a grown man. Well, grown enough to know right and wrong. And if you guys are going after Dawson, then I want in," Jesse pleaded. "You heard what he did to those poor girls. And he killed what? Like, half a dozen men since he's been in town."

"Alright. Dammit," Jed turned and leaned over the porch railing. "We'll ride out at sunrise tomorrow."

"Pack some guns," Bill sat up from his chair and started off. Jed caught him by the arm.

"You keep my brother alive," he said quietly. "Or you won't be getting your pay."

"I can't make that promise," Bill walked away.

Salt River Canyon, 1865

Dawn came over the valley and filled the earth with its warmth. Before anyone else was awake, three riders took off toward the West. They rode north around Crooked Top Mountain and then curved back east to follow the Salt River. In the valley, across the river, there lay a small ranch. Thin fence kept in a modest herd of cattle. The house was adobe build, bleached white by the sun. But the riders hardly took notice. Their eyes were set on something else.

"You think Dawson'll be up by the time we get there?" Jesse asked.

"Doubt it. He don't seem the type to get up early. If'n he is though, he won't be sober enough to shoot straight," Bill called back.

They made steady pace up the banks of the river. Parts were dried up, but deeper pockets still held water, barely trickling downstream. As they got closer to the canyon, the rocks around them started to grow. The river began to wind its way into the mountains, channeling through the sacred rocks. Like most geological features in the desert, the river and canyon showed evidence of massive amounts of water carving through these parts. Water that raged for thousands of years to intricately sculpt miles of dense rock. It's eerie to think that so much destructive power once tore through a world so arid.

The mouth of the canyon was well known by the people in town. The high walls between the mountains narrowed into a deep gorge. Before the mouth, atop a large boulder, grew a lone juniper tree. It was the only growing thing in the ghostly riverbed. Everything else was just sand and rubble.

Bill slowed his horse when he saw the entrance. He pulled out his shotgun and checked to see that the two casings he loaded that morning were still there. He snapped the shotgun closed and then pulled out his pistol. Six bullets filled the cylinder. He flicked his wrist to close the chamber, then holstered his pistol once more. Jesse held two pistols and practiced looking down each of the sights. Jed held his hunting rifle across his lap and waited for the signal to proceed.

"We're sure they're camped at the bottom? We don't want to be ambushed from above," Jesse put his guns away.

"No one camps on a cliffside. Besides, its damn near impossible to get on top of this canyon," Jed looked up the steep walls.

"We should go on foot," Bill swung his leg around and stepped down off the stirrup. "We'll tie the horses to the tree and walk from here. Don't want these girls giving us away."

They dismounted and followed Bill into the tall canyon. They walked through the shallow water, disguising their steps with the little ripples. Their leather boots were tall enough to keep them dry. The sun began to peer over the canyon walls, throwing down rays of light against dark shadows.

Around the bend, they saw the top of a tent just peering over a boulder. Bill crouched and got behind the rock, the others close behind him. Jesse looked at him with anticipation. Bill raised his finger to tell him wait. He kept his back on the rock as looked around the corner. After a quick peak, he saw it was safe enough to take a longer look. A man was sitting at a campfire in his long johns, his back turned to them. There was another tent a little further beyond the one immediately behind the boulder. No one else appeared to be up.

"What is it?" Jed asked quietly as Bill turned back around.

Bill held up one finger and pointed toward the campfire. Jed had clutched his gun when they heard shuffling in the tent behind them. The canvas flaps were pushed open and a man walked out. They heard the footsteps growing closer as the man walked on top of the boulder to take a leak. He froze before he could pull his pants down when he saw three guns pointed at him.

"Taylor!" He yelled to the man at the campfire. Bill blasted him off the boulder, the man falling back onto his tent.

"The hell?" Taylor stood and put on his gun belt and boots. Jesse left their cover and fired at him. The first shot hitting the man in the left arm. Taylor drew and fired but missed when Jesse shot him again in the chest.

"Three to go," Bill said as they advanced into camp. More tents lay further in the canyon. So far, no more enemies showed themselves.

"Dawson!" Jed yelled as he looked around. "Where is Dawson?"

The barrel of a gun poked through one of the tents and fired. The bullet struck Jed in the leg. Bill snapped in the direction and fired. The shotgun spread ripping a hole in the tent.

"You good?" Bill asked as he loaded two more shells into his double barrel.

"Yeah," Jed grunted, examining his leg. "Bullet went straight through." He took his neckerchief off and tied it around the holes in his knee, looking around vigilantly as he did.

"Let's keep moving."

"Two left," Jesse said as they continued around camp.

"Drop your guns," they heard. Dawson emerged from his tent; his gun aimed at the back of Jesse's head. Jed immediately lowed his rifle and set in on the ground. Jesse dropped his pistols on the ground and kept his hands up, never looking back at Dawson. He was a good-looking man, pomade in his hair and a cleanly shaven mustache. A look that the girls fell for, and soon regretted after they saw what an awful man he was. The men in town weren't fooled by his charisma, they all had their encounters with Dawson. He was a snake and there probably wasn't a man in town who didn't want the job of finishing him. But it looked like that was easier said than done.

Bill squinted as he looked around at the scene. The last man of Dawson's gang walked from behind a boulder, aiming his rifle at them. "You, too," Dawson looked to Bill. Though he still didn't move. "I said drop it," Dawson pulled back the hammer of his gun.

Bill slowly set his shotgun down, looking between his two foes. Bill stood quickly and drew his pistol, shooting Dawson down. He turned and shot the last of gang, but not before that man fired on reflex and shot Jedidiah. Dawson and his posse were dead,

"Jed!" Jesse ran over to him. The rifle shot borrowed into his stomach. Blood filling up his clothes.

"Christ," Jed lifted his hands to look at the wound.

"It's not that bad, come on," His little brother held him.

"Shit," Bill looked away.

"Bill," Jed turned his head.

"I thought I could get em both," Bill admitted.

"Don't. You kept my brother safe. That's what I asked of you."

"Can't we take him to the surgeon?" Jesse asked.

"Jesse," Jed turned back to his brother and smiled. "Don't play with guns no more. You hear?" He chuckled.

"No. Come on, Jed," Jesse whipped the tears from his eyes, but his brother was gone.

"Jesse, I'm sorry," Bill squatted down next to him.

"You did this!" Jesse shot up, grabbing his brother's rifle. Bill stumbled back; his hands raised in surrender.

"Now, hold on! Your brother knew the risk he was taking when he wanted to go after this gang."

"You don't care about him! You only wanted the money he was paying you!"

"Don't say that. Now, just lower the gun. Huh?"

"He was my brother," Jesse began to cry.

"I know," Bill sighed and slowly walked toward Jesse. "I know." Bill got close enough to lower the barrel of the rifle, but Jesse.

"He got what he wanted though," Bill continued. "Dawson, his whole gang, they're dead. We got justice."

Jesse nodded and started walking away.

~

They rode back, filling their saddlebags with all the cash and guns they could find in Dawson's camp. Bill let Jesse keep it all, told him he'd be needing it since his brother could no longer work on their ranch. They wrapped Jed in tent canvas and laid him on his horse. The two rode back from the canyon in a weary silence. Only hooves clicking the rocky ground was heard along the river.

Jedidiah Thatcher was buried outside of town, behind the wooden church building. A few graves had already taken up the plot of land since it had been established. Jesse and his mom were there, standing in front of the priest. Bill stood a ways back, smoking a cigarette as he watched.

Boom Town, 1866

The town came together over the past years. All the tents were eventually replaced with wooden structures. The meal tents were about the only portable buildings left, even those were slowly taken over by the cantinas. As they dug the foundations of these rickety buildings, workers uncovered bones in the sand. A mass killing from some forgotten time ago... But among the ivory was always a spec of gold, and so the work would soon continue. Almost everyone found some piece left behind. A few flakes of gold sprinkled into red granite or white quartz was enough to set these settlers on a good start. Even with all the wealth the bank had collected, the three rebels knew they needed to find the mine.

See these pop-up towns were usually founded around mining claims that brought a constant influx of wealth. Jobs were usually secured around the claims and money was made a bit more honestly. This town, however, was built entirely on the sudden and one-time acquisition of wealth. It would work for a while or so, people exchanging the same dollar bills in this isolated economic system. But men, as we know, are never satisfied with holding the same amount of cash day in and day out. Some men are always itching for more. And from what history teaching us about men who always want more, somewhere along the line someone has to pay for it.

"Someone's got to have found a mine by now," Hiram thought aloud. He sat on a table in the bank, eating an apple off a tarnished gold plate with the initials *M.P.* curiously etched in.

"Told you, no one's found nothing," Owen didn't look up from the ledger he was reading.

"You mean to believe all these people keep finding more gold just lying about? Well's run dry; I say," Hiram scoffed.

"I just know people keep bringing in money and that no one's reported to have found a mine. Like here, Doctor Thorne has been making the most deposits, but he certainly doesn't go out in that mountain to dig."

"Even that doesn't add up."

"And why not?" Owen looked up.

"He can't be preforming that many surgeries. Or selling that many tonics. If there's a shooting, it usually results in a death. If anything, the undertaker should be making the money in that situation. It's suspicious," said Hiram

"How is it suspicious? The man makes a decent living. He's a doctor. He probably should be the highest paid person in this town."

"Just check in with him. See how busy he is. People aren't finding leftover gold anymore."

"Suppose it wouldn't hurt. But no one keeps a mine a secret, that's an invitation to getting yourself killed. Reporting your claim and buying it is what keeps you alive and protected by the law," Owen set down his pen.

"The law? *Sure.* Our new marshal does a good job of keeping the law," Hiram scoffed. "Either way though, we need to know if there's a mine out here, so we know how much to invest in this town of ours."

"Alright. I'll check in with the doctor," Owen stood up. He had been wearing nicer clothes ever since he became head of the Golden Field Bank. A new pair of slacks that matched his black vest. His hair was cleaned up with a styled, thin mustache to replace his old messy appearance. A silver pocket watch hung visible out of his pocket, which was worn just for show. Owen had nowhere to be. Any business matters came to him. He had been appraising building projects and orchestrating the layout of his town ever since it all began. They had no mayor, but everyone knew Owen was in charge.

Buildings were set up along a main street with adjacent roads at each end, making a big *H*. The bank had been refurbished. Nice boards replaced the warped planks of the old shack. A big sign was painted and stood on the front wall. It was a black semicircle with white letters. The shakes of the building were freshly painted white which contrasted the heavy black door.

Claude stood security outside. He may not have been very intelligent, but he was a sharpshooter in the war, and everyone knew it. Despite being on the losing side, Claude still wore his old Confederate uniform. The Northern soldiers knew to ignore him when he swore at them, walking by every day. A small dispatch of Union boys was placed here near the end of the war, knowing the town had grown big enough to be of interest. Most folk didn't like the blue-uniformed men patrolling their town, but they had to admit, the soldiers kept them safe from the Apache (which in that day in age, was a big problem).

Claude called after the four soldiers who made rounds down the street. "You boys hear about that Jack Hinson? That man killed over a hundred of yer soldiers. They say he could've won the war by himself!" He never left his chair, only waited for the soldiers to pass by before offering them his thoughts. As Owen and Hiram left the bank, Claude was still laughing at the soldiers.

"...Course you surrendered to us in that battle! You damn cowards! Hell, you didn't need us to kill ya, you couldn't even survive walking through the desert!" They only glared in his direction, never breaking step.

"Leave em be, Claude. You lost," Hiram shook his head as they locked up the bank.

~

Owen went down the road to the doctor's clinic. It was nicest building in the town, for sure. Owen inspected the fine architecture as he walked in. It was only one level, but as wide as the saloon. Nice, polished floorboards met the walls with trim that ran along the floor and ceiling.

"Well, Mister Owen!" Doctor Thorne came from the back room. Under his white stainless lab coat was a fine shirt and bolo tie. From under the front counter, he pulled out a bottle and two fine glasses. "Can I offer you a drink?"

"Why, yes please," Owen smirked and took the glass after it was filled.

"What can I do you for?"

"Just checking in, doc. Making sure you're done building additions to your clinic. How many patients can you hold now? Ten?"

"I got eight beds for recovery and four operating tables for surgery. But yes, I'd say I'm done making additions. Why? Trying to get a loan out of me?" He chuckled.

"No sir. In fact, you haven't taken out a single loan yet. You've been putting money into the treasury throughout your whole construction project."

"What can I say?" Doctor Thorne took a sip of his drink. "I do well. Moving out here was the best financial decision I've ever made. That is, besides investing in medical school."

"The frontier certainly holds great promise of wealth, doctor. Fortune's favored a lot of men out here. But even with our high paying jobs, we know where the real money comes from. Where the money starts."

"And where is that?"

"In the ground, doctor. In the ground. We may be taking in money from the working men of this town, but all their money comes from gold. Hell, that's how I got my start here. But even my luck ran out."

"I'd hardly say your luck ran out, you're among the wealthiest men in town."

"You and me, both then. I've plateaued, though. I stopped finding gold pieces lying around soon after I founded this town. It's been over a year and here you are, still growing in wealth."

"Are you worried I'll pass you? Surely, Mister Owen, medical equipment is expensive. I need to have a good amount of savings for new supplies. On the East Coast, new devices are being produced all the time. If I'm going to keep up with the best medical practices, I need to afford the equipment. Don't tell me you're threatened by my wealth."

"Not at all. Forgive me, doctor," Owen smiled slightly. "It's just that, it's crucial for our town's survival that there is an *income*. People like us are still making money, but if there isn't an influx of wealth for the common man, they'll leave.

You and I both know there hasn't been a mine found in that mountain. A few nuggets pulled from the gulches, but no real mine. My concern, doctor, is that either you are collecting all the wealth in this town—that will eventually drive everyone out—or that you've found the mine that would keep us alive but are hiding it from us. Both endanger the longevity of my town, which I intend to make last."

"Do you suggest I lower the costs of my surgeries? Perhaps lower quality would follow," Thorne set his glass down hastily, some of the liquor splashing out onto the counter.

"No," Owen sighed. "Not at all. I'm just doing my job to keep this town afloat."

"And I will do my job of keeping your people alive. Good day, Mister Owen," The doctor gestured to the door. Owen sighed, set down his unfinished glass, and left.

~

That night, Doctor Thorne left out the back door of his office and covered himself under a wide hat and long coat. In the cover of darkness, he walked behind several buildings before cutting through an alley and crossing the street. He pushed open the double doors of La Taberna and slowly looked at the people in the room. Across the tavern floor he saw a few men sitting at a table, shuffling cards, and counting money. Thorne walked cautiously to the back table and tapped the shoulder of a man. Bill turned to look who had interrupted him but couldn't get in a word before the doctor said, "come with me."

They stepped outside and Bill lit a cigarette.

"What do you need?" Bill asked him behind the tavern.

"You've earned quiet a name for yourself. *Shotgun Bill.*"

"Some people call me that. When there's shooting to be done."

"Well, I need you to be Shotgun Bill."

"Judas priest, Doc," Bill shook his head. "Didn't think men like you got into rough man affairs."

"Usually not. But the founders are out to get me. Owen and his men."

"You know this?"

"Owen stopped by my office today. He knows I'm sitting on a good sum. He's suspicious of me and I fear he's going to send Hiram and Claud out to rob me."

"Why don't you ask the marshal for help if you think you're in trouble?"

"He's not known for getting things done. Besides, I trust you."

"So, what do you want me to do?" Bill blew smoke before taking another drag of his cigarette.

"Get em to back down, stand watch at my door, I don't know."

"You want em dead?" Bill asked.

"Not if we can help it."

"And what's in it for me?"

"The rest."

"The rest of what?"

"The rest of the gold I found."

"So, there *is* a mine?" Bill's face lit up.

"Don't get too excited. I don't know where it is. That Indian you brought to me, he blindfolded me and took me there. Told me I grab all I can as payment for saving his foot."

"How much about is left?"

"Half a bag, there abouts. It's heavy as all hell, I'm sure it'll bring you a good fortune."

"Half the bag bought you your fancy new office, didn't it?"

"I did do some work... but it helped. Do we have a deal?"

"Yeah," Bill flicked his cigarette and shook Thorne's hand. "Yeah, that's a deal."

Shootout on the Mountain

The sun gleamed off the mountain that morning. Hiram walked down the road, still quiet, to the town refinery. More secure than the bank, this place was responsible for trading gold ore into dollar bills. They refined the gold and sent it back east. All money transactions started here. So, if anyone in town had cash, the refinery knew where it came from.

"Morning Hiram," The goldsmith greeted. He wore a light vest over his button-up, sleeves pushed over his elbows.

"Good day."

"What can I do you for? I trust we haven't missed any of our payments," The bank often sent Hiram to collect debts.

"No. Nothing like that," Hiram assured. "We just wanted to double check our records is all."

"Pardon?"

"I was hoping to see your ledger. See there's someone here in town who's been bringing a lot into the bank, we just want to know if that's gold money or not."

"I don't think I can give that information out to you, Hiram," The goldsmith said. Hiram put his hand on his hip, resting atop his Colt revolver.

"I need to see that ledger."

"Hiram, please. I can't give out client information!"

"I just need to know who's been bringing in gold!" They both raised their voices.

"Sir! I can't let you-"

"Give me the God-damned ledger," Hiram drew his gun and pointed it at the man. Two men with rifles came into the room and aimed at Hiram.

"Boys, it's alright. You all can lower your weapons," The goldsmith went over to the back counter and pulled out his ledger. He set the heavy book down on the table next to the balance. Hiram flipped through the logs of who was bringing in how much. Most people brought in only a few ounces at a time, maybe a pound at the most. But every so often there was a transaction of seven or eight pounds, marked under the name of Mr. Thorns.

"Thorns?" Hiram asked.

"Yeah, he comes in here every so often. Says he's a miner."

"Is that so? Did you ask him where his mine is?"

"That's really none of my business."

"No. That is your business! Mines bring in gold, which keeps our town running. It's important we know where that mine is!"

"Look, Hiram, I don't know! I just know mister Thorns comes in here once in a while and drops off some gold."

"Mister Thorns..." He scoffed. "Doctor Thorne is the town surgeon. The man looks the furthest thing from a miner."

"What's it to you?"

"As I said, our town's survival is dependent on finding that mine. We know there's one out here, but for some reason, no one's been able to find it. You better start asking people where they pull their gold from. Otherwise, you and I, and everyone else here will be out of business. And that, is when the shooting starts," Hiram turned and walked out the door. The guards taking their hands of the triggers.

"Find anything?" Owen asked Hiram as he walked into the bank.

"Thorne's been bringing in gold. The damn smith doesn't know from where, though," Hiram shook his head.

"Claude says he's been keeping an eye on his office. He never goes to the mountain. Barely leaves the building, in fact."

"That's cause we're onto him. What does he gain from keeping his mine a secret?" Hiram folded his arms.

"He's probably afraid people will get violent if they find out he's sitting on a gold mine. People killed each other in California for claims. He's not a gunman, he knows he wouldn't survive."

"If he's so defenseless. Who's to say we can't convince him to hand it over to us?"

"You think he would give up the mine?"

"We'll give him a cut of everything pulled out of there. He'll go for it."

"I don't know."

"What?"

"We're putting all of our stock on this one man and the supposed mine he has. We still need other mines to be found to keep everyone happy."

"What do you suggest?"

"I'm not saying we give up on this lead. But we should be incentivizing other miners. Write claims for them, give them legal protection of their mine if they register it."

"We take a cut from those mines, too?"

"Course we take a cut. We're providing 'legal protection.' Tell em it's for paying the marshal or the soldiers. I'll draft up some flyers and get them up around town. Tonight, we'll all pay the doctor a visit."

~

Bugs chirped in the evening heat. Laughing and talking could be heard outside the Taberna and other houses across town. Three men stepped into the street and walked up the sandy path toward the doctor's office. In the cover of night, their faces couldn't be seen. Only their silhouettes against the deep sky gave any hint of their presence. They looked around, making sure they weren't being observed. They didn't notice the man sitting on a rocking chair in front of the office. Not until Bill breathed through his cigar did any light shine on him. His feet were propped up on the railing and his hat covered most of his face.

"Going somewhere?" Bill asked. Hiram and Claude drew their guns on the shadowy figure. "Go ahead, shoot. My reflexes would pull the trigger and I would pelt at least two of you."

"Stay out of this, Bill," warned Owen.

"I know what you're looking for. It ain't here," Bill kept his shotgun aimed at them, holding it across his lap.

"Whatchu mean?" Hiram asked.

"The mine. He doesn't know where it is."

"And you do?"

"Nope," Bill shook his head and blew out a sigh of smoke.

"How can we believe you?" Owen asked.

"You want to know the story? Thorne doesn't know where the mine is cause he was led there under blindfold."

"Bullshit," said Hiram.

"It's true. An Apache led him there. Told him he could grab as much as he could carry, then he was blindfolded again and led out of the mountain."

"Ain't no Apache in this town."

"Not anymore."

"Think we might just ask the doctor ourselves," Claude said. The three stepped toward the door.

"He ain't home," Bill squinted, gripping his gun even tighter.

"So why are guarding?" Owen asked as he opened the door. Bill shot up, but Hiram knocked him back down with the butt of his rifle. Hiram grabbed Bill and dragged him inside, keeping a gun pointed at him.

"Thorne!" Owen yelled. "Claude, get the lantern. Thorne, where the hell are you?"

Claude moved to the counter and lit the oil burning lamp. The building filled with light, illuminating Doctor Thorne in the far room, aiming a shotgun at the men.

"Now, there's no need for that," Owen said coolly.

"Clearly there is, if you went and beat my guard," Thorne didn't take his aim off them.

"We're just here to talk," Hiram said, still holding his gun to Bill.

"Where's the mine, Doc?" Owen asked.

"There is no mine," he answered.

"So where did you get the gold?"

"Found it."

"You found it?" Owen laughed. "Pray tell, where did you just find all that gold?"

"There was abandoned cart. On the trail to Tucson. I went back for supplies after settling here and I found it," Thorne said. Owen turned to Bill, who glared back at him.

"One of you two is lying. Tell me, Doc, how hard is it to do surgery on yourself?" Owen drew his Colt Navy revolver. "Or would you rather reconstruct Bill's face?"

Thorne lowered his gun. Claude jumped over the counter and took the shotgun from him, holding his own revolver out.

"Lead on," Owen said as he pointed his pistol at the door. Thorne walked around the counter, the two men keeping their guns on him. "Keep an eye on him. If he does anything, shoot him."

"You seriously expect me to climb the mountain in pitch black?" Thorne asked them as they walked outside.

"You were blindfolded when you went to the mine. This should be no different," Owen said. "Hiram, watch Bill. We'll be back soon enough."

Thorne started walking. They went out the front door and turned down the alley. He felt the ground begin to slope as he neared the graded mountain side. He avoided the cactus plants with what little vision he had, the other two staying only a few paces behind him. It had been years since he walked into the mountain. He begged his feet to remember. Remember the invisible trail that wove up the mountainside. What if he didn't know the way? Thorne was sweating at the thought. Was it up the rock or further along the shelf? He hadn't noticed he was frozen, without a clue where to go.

Thorne heard the hammer pull back on the gun just behind his ear. Up it was. No time to think if that was the real path or not. He led them uphill, steering around needles and climbing up rockslides. They slowly worked their way up the rock, high above the wooden town below. Crickets chirped at their feet and coyotes howled from the canyon. Claude looked around when he noticed a different sound.

"Keep moving," Owen said, determined to reach the mine. They all stopped when the sound grew louder. A hiss and a rattle unmistakable from anything else.

"Where is it?" Owen asked, not able to see the diamondback rattlesnake.

"There," Claude pointed his pistol to a mass that lay almost disguised as another rock along the trail. The advance must have provoked the snake, as it fired and bit Claude's outstretched arm. He screamed and whipped his arm around until it let go. Both Owen and Claude fired at the fleeing snake. Their guns flashed light on the black mountaintop.

Hiram looked up when he heard the gunshots from the mountain. Peering out the window and wondering to himself if the doctor actually had it in him to fight back or... Bill jumped up and grabbed his rifle, knocking the barrel against Hiram's forehead. They fought for control of the gun, Bill kneeing Hiram in the gut and Hiram elbowing Bill in the head. Bill tackled Hiram and pinned him on the ground, both still holding onto the gun. Hiram tried to aim the gun at him, but Bill moved the barrel downward. It fired and blew a hole in the wall. Bill forced the gun down over Hiram's neck, choking him with it. Hiram threw punches up at Bill, but he took the hits to keep the pressure on him. Hiram coughed and gasped and eventually passed out. Bill got up and kicked him for good measure then ran out the door.

"We have to take him back to my office!" Thorne urged. Claude was on the ground moaning as the venom was already taking its course.

"No!" Owen kept his gun pointed. "You take us to the mine!"

"He's going to die!"

"You want to save him? Lead me to the mine first!"

"What is wrong with you?" Claude looked up at him.

"Shut up!" Owen backhanded him then pointed his gun at Thorne.

"I will take you all back here," Thorne pleaded. "We will find it tomorrow, but right now, he needs help!"

"Claude, start sucking the poison out," Owen ordered. "We're not leaving this mountain," Both men starred at him, now enraged. He pulled Claude up to his feet and pushed him forward. "Now lead on!"

"I'm sorry," Thorne said to Claude as he began walking again.

They neared the top of the mountain and could see the sun beginning to rise. It filled the sky with red and yellow, the stars fading out of view. The doctor began looking around for any opening in the ground. He paced on the mountaintop but saw nothing.

"Where is it?" Owen yelled over.

"It's up here, just spread out and search for it," Thorne replied. The three spread out over the mountaintop, searching among the rocks, in divots, or cracks in the mountain. But nowhere in the pale morning light was there seen, a mine. Owen kept his eye on Thorne, convinced he knew where it was. In reality, the doctor couldn't remember a thing. He had wandered so far on the mountaintop that muscle memory could no longer save him.

Claude was stumbling over his feet. The venom was quickly setting in, causing nausea and deliria. He tripped over a rock and fell to his face. When he looked up, he saw nothing but blackness. Vertigo overtook him as the blackness swallowed him whole. He crawled to his feet, feeling the rock wall around him. Claude threw up then continued onward, deeper into the black tunnel. Wooden beams supported the cave every thirty feet or so. Claude wondered if he'd been swallowed by the snake, the beams turning into ribs in his mind. The cave was like the inside of a snake and the man knew to accept his fate. He shuffled further until his foot hit a large stone. He braced himself on the wall as he lowered himself down to examine what he'd hit. He held the piece up to his face, seeing his reflection in the smooth gold.

"Where's the mine?" He heard Owen demanding the doctor.

"I don't know!" Echoed in.

"I know," Claude whispered to himself. He stumbled toward the light outside. His head getting even lighter, his eyes hurting at the brightness outside. He found a boulder outside and held himself up as he threw up again.

"Found it yet?" Owen turned to Claude. The man looked up and with a smirk, shook his head before throwing up again.

"Dammit," Owen walked away. "I'm losing my patience!"

"I told you, I don't know where it is!" Thorne was sweating with nerves. Owen stormed over and held his gun in the doctor's face.

"You better remember!" His kept hair was now fallen into his face. Owen trembled with rage. His twitching thumb cocked his pistol.

"I don't know," Thorne shook his head. "I don't know!"

Owen turned when he heard, "It's over here!" Bill was standing with his shotgun only a few paces from them. Before Owen could turn on him, Bill fired. The pellets tearing apart his arm. His gun flew from his hand and Owen collapsed onto the ground. Claude began to laugh at the sight, delirious.

"Leave him," Thorne said as Bill turned to him, expecting resistance. "He's dying..."

"It's funny," Claude managed to say. "He didn't care if I died. But *I* found the mine and now," He laughed some more. "I'm taking it with me to the grave."

Bill and Thorne exchanged glances before Claude fell down and, after struggling for a bit, breathed his last.

"And in the grave, that mine should stay," Bill said.

GOLDFIELD

Part 2
The Man

GOLDFIELD

Waltz's Ranch, 1868

They say when a stranger walks into a place, everyone knows he's from out of town. People around stop their talking to size up the new figure in the doorframe and surely, the stranger is looking around at them just the same. New men in town meant new competition, new trouble. A stranger could be anyone, a Pinkerton here to bring justice or a killer on the run. And people will always assume the worse. Jacob Waltz was such a stranger...

"You're not from around here," A man at the bar spoke up, keeping his glass close to his lips.

"Ya know. That's been made clear to me everywhere I've stopped in this state," Jacob walked in and took his hat off. His heavy boots chimed with spurs. He was a dusty old man. Grizzly white beard with thinning hair. He wore a brown duster over his shirt and suspenders. He was lean in frame, but still had some of that "old man strength" to him.

"Then I suppose that means you best move on. We got enough trouble in this town as is."

"Well come on... You wouldn't deny a man a drink, would'ya? Liquor's a human right," Jacob looked to the younger man who began to slowly nod.

"Get this man a drink," He called to the bartender without taking his gaze off Jacob. The older man set his hat on the counter and took a seat on the bar stool as he reached for the offered glass of whiskey. "So, where you from, dutchman?" He asked, recognizing the old man's European accent.

"Not far."

"First time in town, though?" The man at the bar asked.

"Think so," Jacob looked around the building as if trying to remember if he had been there before.

"What brings you in? You curious about city life?" The man at the bar chuckled.

"Hardly."

Not much was said after that. Waltz wasn't a man for giving away information about himself. Lord knows how he made any acquaintances in that town. The man at the bar soon turned to the others sitting at the counter to pick up on whatever they were talking about before Jacob walked in. The old man finished his drink then began looking around the room. He peered over his shoulder, counting how many were behind him. Which ones had guns strapped and which ones did not. He had chosen not to bring his gun into town, wondering if there was a ban, like most places. Now he wondered if he made a mistake.

He'd been in plenty of towns like this out in California. Everyone on edge, everyone's hands floating over their holsters. It was all the same crowd. Men who were quick to start fights, quicker to end a life. Jacob Waltz would look back whenever he heard someone get up. Having his back turned to the room was merely a façade that he wasn't paying attention. When in reality, he knew the key to living out West was always watching your back.

"Howdy, Mister Waltz," Jesse Thatcher walked into the saloon. A few waves were exchanged with the young man. He tipped his hat to one of the prostitutes who winked at him. "Ma'am," He blushed.

"How are you, Jesse?" He asked as the kid sat down on the bar stool.

"Not too bad today. Ma's been packing the wagon. We should be ready to go here in the next few days."

"Where you headin' again?" He asked for sake of conversation.

"Saint Louis. Supposedly there's more work there."

"There's always more work out *there*," He gestured openly. "Everywhere I've gone, it's the same thing: work somewhere else."

"Well, it's not like there wasn't work out here. The ranch paid our dues, but ma and I just couldn't keep up. Getting a smaller place in a real city, that'll be enough for us. I don't know how you manage a herd on your own."

"You just gotta be more stubborn than the bulls, I'd say."

"That, I guess you do. We really appreciate you taking over our herd, by the way. We weren't sure if there was *anyone* in town who knew how to really take care of animals."

"These folks can barely take care of themselves," Jacob scoffed, taking another look around the bar. "I'm just glad your old lady agreed to such a reasonable rate."

"She probably feels bad for you having to take care of those steer all by yourself. There's some stubborn animals in that lot."

"And the horses?"

"We'll probably sell them when we get into Saint Louis. Give us some more to start out with."

"Huh. Did she say if your farmhands would help herd them over to ranch?"

"Yeah. They're all set for tomorrow."

"Good. Your paperwork?"

Jesse pulled from beneath his leather vest, a folded paper. Jacob took it and skimmed the letter that gave him claim to the cattle. In return, Jacob took out an envelope of cash from his coat and slid it over to Jesse.

"Don't lose that," The old man pointed sternly at Jesse.

"Yes sir."

"Good boy," Jacob stood and put his hat on. "Be seeing you tomorrow."

The old man took one last look around the room before he left. His horse was hitched to the post outside the Cantina Roja Inn and Saloon. It was across the street from La Taberna and looked nearly identical. This tavern was owned by a Spaniard, who would often get into quarrels with Roberto, the owner over at La Taberna. Both men arguing in Spanish from across the road over who copied who, whose sign was blocking what view. Despite looking the same, the interiors were two different worlds.

La Taberna was seen as "classy," that is, to the people of Goldfield. It was usually quieter and had a stand-up piano that would play sometimes. Men went here to gamble and make deals and to relax.

The Cantina Roja was a different story. It was rowdy and loud with laughter and yelling. People went here when they wanted to get drunk or get a room with one of the wenches. All around, uncivilized.

Jacob stepped on the sirup and, with a grunt, lifted himself onto his pinto horse. They walked down the street, among other riders and people walking below. The boxy wooden building still looked foreign to Waltz who grew up far across the Atlantic, in Württemberg. The village had color and lay nestled between acres of fresh greenery and rows of flowers and crops.

This land was nothing but brown and beige. Painted buildings were covered in sand and bleached by the harsh sun. The only natural green was cactus and even that wasn't too appealing to the eye. The grass he fed his cattle was dried up and brown. Faint, pale streaks of green ran through the bales of hay as a reminder of greener pastures. Not that the red hue of the land was ugly, most just didn't recognize it.

Jacob rode east out of town and back tracked to the north side of the mountain, which at this point people started to call "The Superstition." Some still referred to it as the Crooked Top, but news about a rumored mine and gunfight spread. Add the mysterious history of a field of gold and bones, where even the Indians were afraid to settle, it practically named itself.

Beyond the Salt River, sat his lone ranch. Jacob's house was adobe, apparently left behind by one of the Pinal Apache. He repurposed the other buildings into storage sheds, keeping his tools and stacks of hay. Around his land was a thin fence that ran down to the river. A modest herd of cattle grazed the valley, looking for traces of grass. The Salt River kept the ground more fertile than could be found on the other side of the mountain. Every day, Jacob would go through his routine of bringing water up from the river, collecting eggs from his chickens, and feeding the cattle and his horse. His morning routine all ended with brewing coffee over the wood-burning stove and watching the sun rise late over the mountain.

It was an honest life that allowed him the kind of isolation he enjoyed. Towns were too full of people for his taste. Too many times, he'd seen people rob and kill one another. As he became increasingly paranoid of his fellow humanity, he decided to go back to the life he had in his home country. But his growing suspicion of men made him just as dangerous as those he feared. He knew the law of the land and so did everyone else: kill or be killed. And he was sure as hell not going to be killed.

~

Before the sun rose the next day, Jacob Waltz was up. He was frying eggs in his cast iron pan, mixed with some diced peppers and onions. The gas lantern flickered in the open house, giving the old man just enough light to eat his breakfast and change into his work jeans. As the sun started to cover the earth, the valley would remain in the shadow of the lonesome mountains.

Soon, Jacob was on the trail and rode into the light, the sun kissed his back with heat. These early mornings were the best times for men of solitude. No one else was up to make a sound, not even the creatures of the earth disturbed the peaceful desert mornings. He rode on for Thatcher Ranch and took in the cool morning air and soft yellow light.

West of town a few miles, was the ranch. The house was built of lumber and shakes, the paint still a pale blue. It was the example of most houses in the West back then. Here today, left behind tomorrow. Right outside the ranch house was a covered wagon, filled with trunks and wooden chairs. All the family belongings and history stuffed into one cart.

Jesse was leaning against the wooden fence, next to a pair of their farmhands. They tipped their hats as Waltz rode in.

"You boys ready?" He asked from atop his horse.

"Sure," One of the farmhands spit out the piece of straw he was chewing. The workers were young men, older than Jesse though. They took the first stable job they could find when everyone first moved into town. Ranching was certainly more honest than most ways people found to earn money.

The two workers with Jesse hopped over the fence and saddled their horses. They rode over to the larger fenced-in area where a herd of about twenty-five was grazing. Jesse dismounted and opened the gate to let the cattle out. The riders then went into the fence and rode around the bunch to herd them all together. The cows grunted and mooed at the action. Riding behind the herd, the cowboys pushed the cattle out of the fence into the open desert. Waltz rode out front to lead the way, riding along the same trail he came by.

"Get along! Come on!" Jesse ordered the cows to keep them moving their steady pace. They chopped the earth with their heavy steps. Dust kicked up into the air and lingered after the herd passed by.

"Oh no you don't," One of the workers rode up beside a cow that was veering away from the herd. The presence of the horse pushed the steer back towards the others.

For the most part the ride over was a breeze. They crossed the river at a shallow point, where the water only trickled through the rocks in the riverbed. Each of the cattle took its time climbing down the bank of the river and up the other side.

The men could see Jacob's adobe house in the distance as they came to the final stretch of the trail. The bright sun flickered behind a shadow on top of the ridge. Jacob stopped to see what it was, thinking someone was on the mountain. But after covering the sun with his hands and squinting to get a look, it was only a lone cactus protruding out from the cliffside.

"Everything okay?" Jesse rode up to Jacob.

"Yeah," He coughed then kicked his horse to keep driving the herd. Up ahead was the fence that surrounded the better half of Jacob's property. Another dozen cattle were grazing the fields down at the river. They began to stir as they saw the new herd approaching. Jacob rode ahead and opened the gates, and the cowboys pushed the cattle into their new field.

"Well, I thank you gentlemen," Waltz tipped his hat to the riders after he closed the gates.

"No problem, Mister Waltz," Jesse replied. "Like I said, we appreciate you taking over the herd."

"Don't mention it. You take care now in the big city."

"Will do," Jesse turned his horse around and kicked for it to start walking again.

"You sure you won't need help out here?" One of the farmhands asked.

"Not a chance," Waltz shook his head.

"Suit yourself," The two workers rode on to catch up with Jesse. Jacob unhitched his horse and walked her back to her stable. Jacob leaned against the fencepost and studied his new herd. He looked up and felt the sun on his face, now high enough in the sky to shine into the valley.

Waltz's Ranch

Storm clouds gathered in the sky. Thunder rang through the air and shook the earth. Jacob Waltz could barely hear his animals over the roaring storm. Lightning flashed over the arid land. After an hour of thunderous display, the rain followed. Those clouds held all the water in territory, some would say. And all of it would be unleashed. Rain pelted the mountain cliffs, streams flowing out of the rocks rushing to the ground. All the runoff flowed into the river, quickly swelling with life.

Rapids started to form down in the canyon. Water crashed around each corner and swamped the boulders that sat along the riverbed. Old tents and rubbish left in the canyon were now swept away, as if the earth were trying to cleanse herself of humanity's stains. Rocks started to loosen with the running water. The sand began to slip, and the stacks began to fail.

Over the continuous thunder, a larger crash filled the valley. Jacob rushed to his back window and peered through the pounding rain. On the far side of the fence, the mountain had crumbled into a rockslide and bridged across the river. A loud cry came from the rockslide and Jacob knew one of his cattle had been caught under the avalanche.

Pulling on his duster coat and boots as he ran outside, Jacob passed through the open field his cows were in. Most were in a frantic huddle, shivering at the rain beating on them with the gusts of wind. As lightning flashed over the sky, he could see how much of the slide went over the river and into his property, destroying near forty feet of the fence. Below the rubble was the back half of a steer, still snorting and pawing the earth with its hooves.

"Easy boy," Waltz got down next to the cow and began to dig with his hands. He threw the rocks behind him, slowly uncovering the bloodied animal. Rain washed the blood down its hind legs and onto the rocks Jacob was digging out. The stones shifted around as the cow grew mad and dug itself further into the earth with each paw.

"Come on," Jacob kept working. Eventually, he removed enough for the cow to stand and run off. It pushed him over backwards into the water that was gathering on the bank of the river. He let out a scream as his back landed on a rock that stuck out from the rest.

"Damn animal," he arched his back and took it out from under him. He sat for a bit in the water, holding the rock in his hand as he felt the ache in his back. His thumb moved along the grooves and indents that marked the peculiar stone. He looked down at it, seeing the stone had been carved with lines. He carried it with him as he went back inside and he never stopped looking at it.

Waltz turned his boots over as he walked in the door. Water splashed out over the hardwood. His coat was drenched and trailed water as he threw it off. Jacob had almost forgot to shut the door, closing out the storm. Shivering, he moved to light the wood-burning stove. He flicked his lighter until a flame was sustained. He moved the lighter into the stove and lit some of the twigs beneath the chopped logs. A faint orange light flickered and radiated out into the dark room. He flipped the steal lid of the lighter shut and held his hands over the flame. Jacob then sat down on his kitchen chair and took off his wool socks, completely soaked through. He sat there for a moment, catching his breath, and warming himself up. He dozed off as he looked across the room to the carved rock that sat on the kitchen table.

~

The next morning was calm, clouds were still receding from the sky. Jacob Waltz woke up cold in his clothes. The stove had burnt out a few hours past midnight, after Jacob had fallen asleep on his chair. After he got up and changed, Jacob went outside to assess the damage. More of the cliffside had collapsed than he thought. He grumbled to himself as he saw a few of his cattle outside the fence, grazing on the freshly watered ground. The chicken coop was swamped. Pools of water stood where the earth was traditionally cracked dry.

He spent most of the day removing rock from his side of the bank. The sun beat on him as he shoveled rocks into a wheelbarrow, sometimes having to lift the larger stones one at a time. It helped that the river was running high, the water passed through the rockslide and pushed a lot of the smaller rock further downstream. The fence beneath the rubble was broken and beyond repair. Jacob feared the worst: he'd have to go to town again. There was no way he could make do with the lumber he had. The old man grumbled under his breath at the thought.

Going back inside, he grabbed a bag of dollar coins and his hat. He hitched his horse up to a small cart and whipped the reins for it to begin walking. Jacob took the far way out of his ranch, trying to push the free roaming cattle back home. Yet they remained fairly unphased.

The cart bumped over the rocks and sank into the mud as it went along. Jacob stopped when he reached the river crossing, that was now much wider and presumably deeper. He waded out into the flowing river, the water reaching the top of his thighs.

"Alright, girl," He patted the horse on the neck. He climbed aboard cart, grunting as he pulled himself up. He clicked his tongue and whipped the reins lightly. Slowly, they crossed the river. Water flowed under the horse's belly and through the spokes of the wagon wheels. The horse quickly pulled itself up onto the bank and snorted as she had to take the cart out with her.

"Come on, now," He flicked the reins to spur her on. After a few powerful steps, the horse had pulled them out of the riverbank. They continued down the trail that looped east into town.

The lumber yard was on the other side of the town, on the southeast corner of the H-shaped streets. Logs were hauled in from the South and the forests found in the North. Most store owners that moved into the town brought their modular shops with them, hauling the wooden walls from town to town. But if anyone intended to build here for good or hope to improve their structures, they needed more lumber. It was a valuable resource this far out in the desert, for none of the white men knew how to make houses from adobe like the Apache in the territories that surrounded them.

Jacob Waltz was no carpenter, but building a fence was simple enough. He bought a pile of 4 by 4's to make the posts and a few 2 by 6's to make the rails. He got a box of heavy nails from the town blacksmith, who was usually busy producing picks and shovels.

"Planning on digging out the mountain?" Jacob scoffed as he saw the stockpile of mining tools.

"Ain't you hear? The bank's put up a reward for anyone who finds the gold mine 'round these parts. Folk been coming in from all over to look for it," The smith replied. He was a bigger man with a greying black beard and balding head. "Business has been good," He smirked.

"Fool's errand," Waltz shook his head. "Ain't no real money in gold. Maybe one in the whole town will get rich, but I'd hardly call that a living."

"Towns don't spring up for anything else," The smith chuckled.

"Don't close for anything neither," Jacob took his box of nails to leave.

"You have a good day now."

Jacob tipped his hat as he was on his way out the door.

After clearing away the rubble from his side of the river, he dug new post holes and drove the 4 by 4's into the dirt. He took a sip of water from the flowing river before continuing on, cupping it in his hands and splashing his face. He nailed the boards to the fence posts and not long after, the fence was back to new. He sat down and leaned against the fence. Catching his breath in the dry heat, burning his leathery skin. Looking out to the desert, he saw a few of his cattle roaming about. He grumbled in frustration before getting up.

"Damn animals."

He spent the better part of that evening wrangling the loose cattle. He rode around them, his horse chopping the earth as he worked to steer the cows back toward the ranch. The air was hot as he worked in the golden hours. The hard labor was almost exhilarating to him. Jacob had years of herding cattle under his belt and certainly spent many long hours tracking down strays. Some people even say that roping cattle was the only thing that could make the old grouch smile. The rush of riding a horse, sprinting to catch their chase, was pure thrill to an old cowboy like Waltz.

Shootout at Goldfield, 1889

"Never thought we'd see this town get a second wind," Bill said as he sat on the cantina porch. Over the last twenty years, cowboys and rustlers and all sorts of characters had moved into the town. Most heard of the bank's incentive to find a mine, others were just looking to settle in a promising town.

Hiram was the last of the founders left to run the bank and watch over the town. Bill had left him alive the night the founders took Doctor Thorne up the mountain. He had always wondered if that was a mistake, if Hiram would come for revenge after all this time. The longer Bill was in the business of being the town mercenary, the more he feared being the next target.

Hiram had made the decision to formally establish the town in order to save it from abandonment. A post office was built off the main street. A mayor came in from the East and built his office as the second level to the bank, seeing it as the most secure building in the wild town. Mayor Weathers was a shrewd man, serving on boards all over the west, trying to save boom towns from going under and become more permanent. The incentive to find the mine brought new folk to the town, but still kept the whole economy hinged on one industry. "It simply wouldn't do," as he said.

The first thing the mayor instated was to give the town an official name. People called it by many things over the years, but more often than not this boom town was referred to as Golden Field, after the bank. That name was often cut down in the shorthand way of speech that everyone talked with. So, when reports were going around about an incentive to find a mine, the name people heard was "Goldfield."

Though, not only the mayor was called in to keep the town from running itself in the dirt. That good-for-nothing marshal was replaced with the first real sheriff. As always, Bill declined the position when it was offered to him. He cared for justice, but not for government authorities. Instead, a man from Phoenix came down to take up the star.

Durant was his name. He was a tall man with blonde hair kept back under his cowboy hat. Bristles lined his chin. He wore the brass star over his heart as he walked around town. His spurs chiming with each step. He had a pistol strapped to his hip, but he rarely had to use it. He wore a light button-up shirt, tucked into his worn jeans, kept under a shinning belt buckle. His bright blue eyes were like the pale sky above them, shining out from under the shade of his hat.

"I would have liked to've seen this place before," Durant said, sitting next to Bill, with his feet propped up on the railing outside La Taberna. Even with his distaste for U. S. officials, Bill was drawn to Durant. He was a calm man and often sought Bill for help as he got on his feet.

"There wasn't much to see. Can't say places like this ever see their heyday," Bill spat, then kept on his chewing tobacco. He was in his upper forties now.

"Maybe not. But they sure see their dark days."

"You're sounding like the preacher."

"Even he gets one right every now and then," Durant chuckled. "I don't much like this gold mine business."

"You and me, both. You didn't see the bloodshed it caused before. Now that riders are coming in from all parts of the territory..." Bill paused. "Well, I don't know. Nothing good can come, that's for sure."

"People may move out here for the gold, but if they want to avoid dying out here, they need to find another way of life."

"Easy for you to say when you're paid by our taxes. Not everyone has that luxury."

"Don't bullshit me, Bill. No one here pays their taxes," Durant shook his head with a smile. "I hope Weathers knows what he's doings. Trying to turn a ghost town into a thriving place is a helluva job."

"Don't get your hopes up. You may have landed a stable job, but this town's a powder keg. People are getting itchy for money. And when everyone's out hunting the same thing, they'll do whatever they can to keep the other guy from getting it."

Durant was about to reply when they heard shouting across the street. From the Cantina Roja, a man was thrown out the double doors. He hit the wooden stairs, then tumbled backwards into the street. Standing in the doorframe was a man with his pistol drawn. He stepped out from the shadow into the light. This man had jet black hair and bright eyes. He had a bolo tie around his neck and scars on his forehead.

"Paul! Please," The man on the ground called as he crawled backwards across the sand.

"Git up," Paul Harris pulled him by the collar onto his feet then pushed him away.

"I swear, I didn't know!" He pleaded.

"*Didn't know* my ass! You don't cross one of my boys and expect to get away with it!" He yelled as he walked back a few paces. Durant was about to get up to intervene when Bill caught him and shook his head without a word. Durant slowly sat down and watched.

"I didn't know he was one of your guys, honest. Just... Just let me go."

"I oughta kick your teeth in so you can hear how stupid you sound," Paul put his pistol back into its holster, but kept the hammer cocked. On his other hip, was another cattleman revolver. He eyes narrowed onto the man, still shaking with fear. By now, the streets were cleared. Men stood around to watch, but only from a distance. "You run, I put a bullet in your back. The only way out is to face me. That's the penalty for cheating my men."

The man didn't reply but kept his hand trembling over his own holster. The sun was in his eyes, too. He knew he must have lost his hat when he was first confronted in the Cantina. Paul slowed lowed his hands, now resting on his pair of six-shooter guns. They stared each other down for a moment.

Then they drew.

Three shots were fired in rapid succession. At the end of it all, Paul stood over the man he'd thrown out in the street. Durant's eyes widened and leaned forward to grasp what he just saw. Bill was still reclined in his chair. He'd seen Paul duel before.

"Get this filth out of here," Paul called to a few of his gang who were standing by the Cantina. The pair came and dragged the body down the road toward the mortician. As the corpse went by, most people turned away. But Durant looked on to see one bullet hole in the man's chest.

"You catch what happened?" Billed asked quietly, knowing for himself.

"He missed the first shot," Durant mumbled as he was still trying to run the events in his head.

"Paul doesn't win duels because he's good," Bill stood up. "He's a poor shot. He wins by disadvantaging his opponent as much as possible. But people see him walk away and know none the wiser. His first pistol is just a distraction."

"How long have you been watching him?"

"Few months," Bill got up and started walking slowly into the street. Durant followed. "His crew moved into the area, oh, awhile back. The Varmints, they call themselves."

"I've heard of them over in Phoenix," said Durant. "Didn't know who they were really."

"Thieves. Gamblers. Murderers. Just a crew of men trying to muscle all the money they can get. They ain't more complicated than that, I'd say."

"So, why not ride out against them?"

Bill laughed. "No. You don't 'ride out' to bring them down. Their posse now is nearing twenty-five strong."

"There must be some way."

"Like I say, I've been watching them for months. Trying to find out as much as I can. So far, no way I can see to get them out."

"They really *are* varmints."

~

Paul rode out of town with two others riding behind him. They went east and up the hills below the Superstition Mountains. Their camp was set up at the bottom of a steep cliff. Inscribed on the face of the cliff were paintings left behind from long ago Apache. The faded red and black marks went down into a cave, hallowing the base of the cliff, where a small stream trickled past. A single adobe house was left in the back of the cave, where Paul lived. The rest of the Varmints set up tents surrounding the area. They had a wire coop for chickens and a wide fenced in area for their horses. Carriages and covered wagons were parked next to the tents, their contents spilling out on the ground around them. Their camp wasn't hidden, but no one dared try to take them.

Twenty-five men made up the Varmints. Several of the men brought their wives along and other girls that ran with the gang and worked as wenches in the local cantinas, picking pockets and noting which travelers would be good targets to rob out on the trail. Somehow, these ladies were the most civilized of the group.

What was unknown to the men of Goldfield, was that this gang was a collection of the territory's most wanted. Majority of the men had been in prison together, rotting away in the desert's most secure prison. Mogollon Rim, *Hell on a Mountain.* In the northern part of the Arizona Territory, high up in the mountains, these murderous men were all sentenced to death. Only, the prison warden prolonged their executions, wanting to break each one of them first. Confined to their own stone cells, the men grew mad. They were treated like animals so many of them became like animals.

Paul was among the few who kept a cool head. He knew there was nothing he could do but wait. Not giving the guards any satisfaction, they kept him alive to see what it would take to finally break him. Sometimes, the guards would take him into the yard and whip him, other times they would try to starve him out, not giving him any food or water. Most of all, Warden Koch loved to strut by his cell and taunt him, wearing shiny black shoes and two polished revolvers on his hips.

"Just say the word and I'll end you right now. Shoot you down like all the *varmints* in this jail," The warden would aim his six-shooters into the dark cell. "Pew," He pretended to shoot. His crooked grin shadowed by his wide hat. But Paul would never give him a reaction. He simply waited. One day, his patience paid off.

In the middle of the night, fire was seen over the mountain top. Guards in the fort rushed to grab water, but it was no wildfire. Geronimo had come. He and his men carried torches in one hand and axes or guns in the other. He was an old man, grey hair tied into a ponytail, but his eyes were fierce with life. The fire grew bright and burned on the mountain. The whoops and howls came from the Apache as they drew ever near. Over the shouting chorus, the guards heard "Geronimo!" and were struck with fear. The Apache seemed to them like black ghosts in the shadows of the fire they carried.

Before they could come back to their senses, Geronimo's men were upon them. Guards were shot off the square watchtowers and torches were thrown at the gates. The Apache rushed the fort and the fire blazed behind them. They threw their torches at anything not made of stone. The fight ensued as the guards began to fire back, but they were greatly outnumbered. Tomahawks and bullets sliced the air and picked off men on both sides.

The fire quickly spread over the arid ground. Tents, carts, and men all caught flame. The fire spread next to the powder kegs, and then the night exploded. Blasts shook the earth and blew in the stone walls. The dark sky smeared across with orange and red.

Blasts had torn open some of the jail cells. Other men were reaching through the bars to try and grab the keys off a fallen guard. Eventually, the prisoners were loose and entered the fight.

The Apache had it in mind to kill every man in that fort, but they stopped when they saw the prisoners attacking their captures with primal ferocity. Some men armed themselves with bricks to beat in the guards, not having any guns. Others wrestled on the ground, trying to choke and punch and kick their way to freedom. Paul stood in the chaos and watched the scene. He scanned over the fight until he saw the warden, defending himself with dual pistols.

Pulling an axe from one of the dead Apache, Paul trudged through the fight, walking over the burning ground to the warden that had tortured him for years. Koch turned and grinned as his foe walked toward him. He aimed and fired. But the hammer fell with just a click. Terror filled his eyes.

"Years you've been waiting to shoot me, and now you're out of bullets," Paul said, glaring at him. Koch holstered his weapons and raised his fists. Paul swung the axe, but the warden blocked his arm and threw a left hook in return. Paul slashed upward, cutting the warden's face. Koch put his hand to his mouth, seeing the creases in his palm fill with blood. Paul brought the axe around again, but Koch caught his hand and twisted the axe out of his hand. They exchanged punches, each man taking his time between blows. The fire burned around them even further, charring the adobe fortress. Their sweat nearly burning off their skin in the heat.

Paul punched the warden in the jaw, a tooth flying from his mouth. Koch swung back and laid Paul on the ground. He went to reach for the axe, but Koch stomped on his hand. Paul yelled out in pain. He rolled over and took the axe in his left hand. Swinging across, Paul chopped through Koch's knee, crippling him on the ground. Paul crawled on top of him, Koch reaching up to strangle him. He punched Koch with his right, but screamed himself when he realized it was broken. Koch laughed through his bloody teeth, still limp on the ground. Paul quickly turned back and brought the axe down on his foe.

Geronimo looked onto Paul for a moment then turned his forces away without a word. Left in the fire were twenty men, liberated from their bondage. Like wolves starved and beaten, then suddenly unchained. Without knowing what else to do, the escaped prisoners stole the guard's horses and guns and anything else they could find and rode off.

Paul grabbed the warden's pair of cattleman revolvers and secured them around his waist. But with his broken hand, he lost his ability to shoot straight. No matter how long he practiced, his right hand could no longer hold steady. He set up empty bottles and practiced his draw with the two guns, but his right would always miss. Eventually though, Paul could aim with his left and shatter every bottle he set out. As quickly as he could shoot again, he was riding out with the newfound posse. Rage burned in them, they lusted for revenge on the world that had put them behind bars. They rode along the coach roads and robbed anyone who crossed their path. They steaked out near Phoenix for a while, taking everything they wanted. More ruffians eventually joined their crew, wanting to take part in their fight for riches and their war against justice. Then they heard of Goldfield and the flood of men looking for that mine. They moved to the East side of the Mountain and brought even more trouble than that town generated for itself.

Mayor Weathers had grown so concerned about people moving out because of this gang, he promptly booked a band of the same name to come a play. That way if anyone asked about the Varmints, he could say,

"I'm excited for them to come to town. You better stick around to hear them. Their music is simply exquisite!"

Lord knows if that was the best way to handle an outlaw problem.

The Mine

Jacob Waltz sat in his house one afternoon and stared blankly at the stone he'd pulled from the river. One marking resembled something like a cactus on a cliffside. There were a few arrows with some *X*s between a few other lines. The long-forgotten stone was a tribute to the devil's handiwork in this story. What was lost and buried with the dead had now revealed itself again. And to the perfect victim. He stared at the stone until he started to recognize the shape of the cliffside with a single cactus growing out from it. He'd only passed by that cliff a dozen times as he'd gone to and from the town.

Jacob secured his leather belt around his waist and spung the chamber of his six-shooter to double check it was loaded before sliding it into the holster. In his worn knapsack, he packed some rope, fire starters, and an additional box of ammo. He threw on his duster coat and large round hat and pocketed the stone as he left his adobe.

He rode out along the trail, already scorched dry from last week's storm. The sun was bright against the pale, sand earth. It burned on his face as he rode. His horse kicked up dust as it galloped along. Coming around the bend, not too far from his ranch, a small cliff stuck out from the rock wall. He rode past it and turned around to see the edge of the cliff mirroring the rock's carvings. He compared the ridgeline to his stone map.

"Would you look at that," Jacob chuckled to himself. He looked at the stone and studied the other markings. Trying to find them on the mountain side, he looked between the two until he noticed the subtle trails snaking their way along the cliff.

Kicking his horse to begin walking again, he got right up the river across from the cliff, trying to find a way to get up to the trail. It seemed to just start at the lone cactus and take off from there. He certainly couldn't out right climb to it, not in his age at least. He traced the ridge of the cliff until his eyes came to a cave. Slowly walking his horse, he followed the base of the mountain until he saw another cave opening, lit up by the evening sun. From the mouth of the cave, the trail picked up and worked downward. He rode his horse across the river and followed the trail until it came to a washout. 'The debris might just be enough,' He thought.

Jacob got off his horse and put the lead under a large rock to keep her from wandering off. He took off his duster and rolled up his sleeves as he got up to the landslide. The large pieces of the mountain stacked on top of each other like a giant staircase. Jacob looked around, but there was no one in view. He pulled himself up and onto the first boulder. He looked up the landslide and shook his head at how far he had left to go.

He groaned with his aching knees and huffed with each step. Some rocks wabbled beneath his feet, others were firmly stacked and gave him checkmarks to rest at. Climbing over the fallen rocks, he worked his way up to the trail. It was thin and partially washed out, but it was a trail, nonetheless. He kept his back against the cliff face as he sidestepped his way along the trial. The loose, dry rocks beneath him would sometimes slip and tumble off the mount. His breath became short, trying not to look down the sheer cliff.

The trail widened out by the cave entrance. It was black on the inside, but a sliver of light came from within. Jacob pulled himself up into the cave and sat for a moment to let his eyes adjust. It was just tall enough for him to get through, but it was admittedly rather skinny at some points. He started again, carefully seeing where he placed his feet. As he worked to slide through a narrow point, he stopped in horror of what sat right in front of his face. The shiny black body took slow steps, turning to face him. Its pincers could almost reach out and touch his face. The scorpion's tail could almost certainly strike him if it wanted to. Shivers shot through his spine at the realization that he had no idea what was on the wall behind him. Jacob gulped and slowly shifted through the pass.

Getting to the light at the other side of the tunnel, he searched himself, looking over his shoulders to see if anything had clung unto him. He worked to shake off the creepy crawling feeling that hadn't left him. He looked up to see the lone cactus sticking out from the cliffside. The spiney plant was a welcomed sign that he was on the right track. He took out the stone again and traced the markings with his finger. The trail veered up in a zig-zag pattern, diverting from the ridgeline itself. He followed his map, up the unassuming trail. The switchbacks climbed higher to the flat summit of the mountain. Where trail met the mountain top, a large stone sat against the darkening sky. By this time, the sun had dipped below the horizon, reds and purples bleeding into the sky. The navy sky was dotted by bright white lights, twinkling above. Jacob wondered at the lone rock, purposefully placed at the crux of the trail. He rolled it over, the flat bottom now pointing up. He felt grooves carved into it, like the ones on the first stone map.

Hastily, he pulled the matches from his backpack and struck one. The fire ignited brightly and dimmed to a steady burn. The light revealed the map on this forgotten stone. It was the shape of the mountain from the top with large landmarks carved into it. Rock stacks and divots all placed in relative scale. Through these geological features, was a long trail that cut across the mountain top. It started where Jacob was standing and ended at what looked like a cave. He flicked his wrist to blow out the match then started to walk the course that was laid out.

"Let's see," He mumbled to himself as he approached one of the rock stacks, trying to remember where the map went next. He wove around the rocks until he saw the spot where the trail ended. It was an abyss that seemed to dive to the heart of the mountain. Cold wind blew from it, with a low moan. Jacob shuttered at the thought of it. He drew his pistol and pointed it into the darkness. With his left hand, he struck another match and started inwards. The cave was black all around. The appearance of wooden beams spooked him, like the ghost of something long ago. A ghost of something not quite right.

Jacob saw a rusty lantern on the ground and bent down to light the wick. It caught flame and burned what little oil it had left. The dirty glass illuminating the flame brighter to fill the cave. He carried it with his gun still outstretched as he went deeper into the abandoned mineshaft. Soon, light began to sparkle off the walls and ceiling. The further Jacob went, the brighter the lights would be. He walked until he heard a crunch. The old man lifted his boot to see a caved-in skull partially buried in the ground. He looked at it only for a moment before his eyes became distracted by the glittering lights around him. He left the skeleton as he kept going into the cave. The light around him burned from the veins of ore wrapping themselves around the mine. The gold's cold fingers wrapping around Jacob Waltz, totally bewitched by the sight.

~

Along the washouts and ruts, men were on their knees or wading out in the streams. With their hands, they picked through granite and quartz. Others took pans and sifts, scooping the river bottom. There were always men who got easily discouraged by the endless search for gold. It wasn't hard to look over your shoulder and see the tall cantina signs. But those who stayed out in the heat, sifting pan after pan, were the ones rewarded for their monotonous work. For every once in a small while, a spec of gold would shine through the mud.

One of the miners even found a little vein. He was a skinny man with a lazy eye and even poorer teeth. Streaks of gold ran through the red rock on the banks of the dead river. He got down on his stomach to cover his find as he chipped a few nuggets away from the granite. He looked over his shoulder to see if anyone had noticed what he'd discovered. He pocketed the gold and stood up; his head barely poked out from the riverbed.

"A claim. I need to get a claim," he thought. started to walk away, but quickly turned back to see the little vein shimmering in the light. He walked back to the vein and kicked some dirt over it, then proceeded to walk away.

Turning back again, he was nervous his find would still be discovered. He bit his nails and looked around him. He saw men further down the riverbed and along the base of the mountain and a couple walking towards him. He went back to the vein, untied his trousers, and then pissed on the rocks. The couple of men walked by with panning tools, but kept walking as they saw this man relieving himself in the gulch. They rolled their eyes and kept walking. Satisfied with his defense, he quickly gathered his tools and hurried into town.

The miner joined the other men lined up outside the goldsmiths to get their nuggets weighed and paid for. The cash didn't last long though, it usually ended up washing down some bottle. If you were smart, you turned your cash into tools to help you dig more gold. But few men were smart.

Jacob Waltz stopped along the road when he saw the long line of prospectors outside the goldsmith. He scowled at the thought of having to stand around a crowd of people. Resting his hand on top of his holster, he peered around town to see if there was anywhere else he could make his transaction.

"Buddy, if you aren't going to wait, you best just move on," A man said as he stepped into the line in front of Jacob.

"Is there anywhere else to get gold exchanged around here?" Jacob asked while he was still looking up and down the store signs.

"I guess so," The man thought. "Thomas's General Store has a scale, but no one rightly goes there."

"And why not?"

"Suppose you'll see for yourself, won't ya?" The man laughed as he turned around to keep his place in line.

Jacob shook his head and walked down the dirt road to Thomas's General. For the usual activity around town, the building looked abandoned. He pushed open the free-swinging door and stepped into the shadowed room. The sun outside only peered through the wooden shakes over the windows and cracks in the ceiling. The floorboards were covered in dirt and most of the stock was coated in a fine layer of dust. The inventory was fairly standard, food and feed, picks and pans, and a whole assortment of elixirs and ointments.

"You lost?" A dark woman behind the counter asked. She was near thirty and fairly strong.

"Don't reckon I am," Jacob continued in, pointing at the gold scale. "I need to get some gold exchanged."

"I see," she said, surprised. "Not many folk shop here cause they don't like the idea of a woman owner her own shop. Not a woman of color, no less."

Jacob grunted in reply.

"Didn't think people would even allow it," She continued. "But I'm glad you've come to be wiser."

"Now don't think I'm some sort of idealist," The old man raised his hand to stop the woman, who clearly hadn't spoken to someone in a while. "I just hate all people equally."

"Suppose that'll do," The chatty woman moved to the scale, bringing an oil-burning lamp to help see. "Julia's the name. Julia Thomas. Most folk only know me as the worker here before Mister Thomas died. But they never knew we was married. I actually-"

"Jacob," The old man introduced himself as a means to get her to stop talking.

"Pleasure to meet ya. Now, let's see that gold." Jacob removed his worn backpack and set it on the counter. He looked over his shoulder for good measure before taking out two large pieces of gold. The heavy stones were each bigger than a fist. "Christ almighty," Julia said under her breath. "This is real?"

"Yes, ma'am," Jacob assured. "I tried to chip away most of the quartz, there. But otherwise, that's solid gold."

"Where did you ever find these?"

"I'd rather not say actually. But if you don't mention these to anyone, I'll consider bringing my business back here in the future."

"Fair enough," She put one of the ore pieces on the scale. It tipped instantly. Julia moved the sliding weights to balance the scales. Then she took out an ink pen and notepad to scribble down the weight and calculate how much it was worth. She did all that once more for the second piece of raw gold, mumbling to herself as she did the math.

"Alright, Mister Jacob. At sixteen dollars an ounce, you made quite a pretty profit today. Actually, more than I can pay you right now."

The old man looked around as he thought.

"I'll take what you can give me. You can keep half of your cut. I'll also take the tools I need to get more, as insurance I'll get the rest when you send those to the coast. *Then* you can take your second half of the cut."

"That sounds reasonable," Julia went for the lock box and counted out five one-hundred-dollar bills. "Should I tell them to be expecting more large orders, then?"

"It wouldn't hurt to mention it," Jacob put the cash into his jean pocket. He grabbed a lamp and a canister of oil to put into his backpack. Then he took a pickaxe and hoisted it over his shoulder. "Oh, and one more thing," Waltz stopped in the doorframe. "If you tell anyone who I am. I'll kill ya."

Julia gave out a terrified chuckled, but the look on Waltz's grizzly face told her he wasn't joking. Julia gulped and nodded. And with that, Waltz left.

That night Julia put the ore into a wooden box and nailed the lid shut. She held the box under her coat as she walked out into the dusty streets. A lot of people were still awake, walking to and from the taverns at night or just sitting on their porches. But no one paid any attention to her. She slipped into an alley and walked around to the back side of one of the stores. This side of the builds were unlit and often unseen. She looked over her shoulder before knocking on the back door. After a few moments, the goldsmith opened the door just a sliver.

"What? Oh, Mrs. Thomas..." He noticed who it was right away. He had done business with Mr. Thomas when he was still alive. They often shipped their gold ore together to save on extra wagons carrying their valuables.

"I have some ore to add to your next shipment. Whenever the coach comes through again," She spoke quietly.

"There isn't much to add to, we haven't been doing too well as of late," The goldsmith replied. "But we'll send what you have regardless."

~

By early that next year, the first batch of Jacob's gold had reached the Bank in San Francisco. The Wells & Fargo Company wagon had come and gone and brought money back to Mrs. Thomas to repay Jacob for what she owed.

Waltz returned to the mine on a more regular basis. He was careful to go in the dark of night. Sometimes he would wonder if the stars were too bright and maybe he'd be seen. Often his desire to keep digging would outweigh his fear of being seen. Not that he wasn't afraid of being caught. When he walked the trail, his head turned more than an owl's. His hand ever-resting on his gun belt. Even when he was at home, he never took his gun off. The only time he wasn't looking over his back was when he would reach the gold vein. Then all of his conscience was consumed by the streaks of gold that glittered in the darkness.

In spite of his best efforts. There was one person who noticed Jacob's coming and going. On the north side of the ridge, a man sat in a tent, studying the mountain top during the day. At night, he'd seen Jacob's silhouette scrambling up the trail and move over the top of the ridge. In the morning, the man followed Jacob with his binoculars as he worked his way down the northern face of Superstition Mountain and disappeared from sight. This man set his binoculars down and took a drink from his canteen, all with his left hand. He picked the binoculars up again when Jacob and his horse rounded the bend again to go to his ranch. This man pushed himself to his feet with his left hand, for nothing but a stump remained of his right, which was wrapped and held in a sling.

He walked out of his tent and felt the wind and sun on his face. His black hair and mustache were grown and unkept. His once clean vest was scuffed up and stained. The man reached across his waist and drew his Colt Navy revolver from its holster, which was designed to be on his right side. And standing on the top of the mountain, he stretched his arm out, practicing his aim with his left hand. It shook with rage as he glared down the sights. His hand trembling with rage.

Goldfield, 1890

Hiram sat in the bank office at night. His lamp burned faintly in the dusty room. Business in town had picked up, so no one would have ever suspected that the bank wasn't doing well. Most of the money it owned had been loaned out to people who hadn't returned on their investments. But Hiram kept track of the place all the same. He thought often about that night on the ridge. Course, he wasn't there. He had to hear retellings by people in the saloon, each of them exaggerating some amount of his friends' deaths or adding their own twist to the story. It gave his imagination somethin' to run with. Claude being bitten by a rattlesnake made since to him. He had always been a clumsy fella, it surprised Hiram that it didn't happen sooner. Then of course, Owen got himself blown to shreds. Shotgun Bill tore off his whole arm they said. Probably wasn't long before he bled out. Suppose he had it coming, too. Some said they found the mine somewhere between those events.

"Maybe," the ex-rebel thought, but he wasn't going to go after it no more. He was alright with just quietly living on, not causing more trouble. He could've died in the war, could've died that night by Bill's own hand. But he didn't. And he wasn't going to find no more reasons to introduce himself to Death. He didn't even a gun anymore. Nope. Hiram sat safe in his bank, looking over ledgers. Seeing who owed what and figuring who he could probably squeeze the money out of.

The wooden floor creaked as a figured stepped inside. Whether Hiram had been zoned-out or whether he realized that quickly that the door had been locked, didn't matter. Hiram just about fell off his chair when he saw just who was standing before him. The man's right hand was wrapped and held tight to his chest. In his left was a pistol. It wasn't even his ghostly appearance that spooked Hiram to the ground. It was the fact that he was looking at a man who had been presumed dead.

"Owen? Y-you died," Hiram gasped. He looked rougher than what he looked in the war, but it was unmistakable.

"Hiram," he said as he walked further into the bank. The man on the ground scurried back, still thinking this might be a phantom here to haunt him for their unfinished business. I found it."

"What?

"I found it," he said again. "I found it!"

"The mine?" Hiram sat up.

"I know where it is. There's a man who comes and goes and comes and goes. And I found it!" Owen stepped closer.

"Okay," Hiram was catching his breath, taking in a mix of emotions.

"We need to get it!" He said with a trembling smile. "We need-"

"Owen... no."

"What did you say?"

"We're not dying for that stupid mine. It's not worth it."

"It's worth everything!" he shouted. Hiram realized how tightly Owen was holding his pistol. His index finger, hovering over the trigger. "I've watched the mountain and I found it!"

"I hear you. But we're not going after that again."

"Yes, we are. We're going to find that man and we're going to kill him and that mine will finally be ours!"

"Owen," Hiram thought quick. "It's done. Someone found the mine. It's-"

"Did he register it?"

Hiram was caught speechless.

"Did he fucking register it?"

"No, dammit!"

"Then we still got a problem."

"No, we ain't," Hiram pushed himself to his feet. "We're not going after that mine."

"I was left for dead on that God forsaken mountain. No one ever came to look for me."

"I'm sorry!" Hiram blurted. "I was told you were dead. I wasn't ever gonna be able to find you in those mountains!"

"Shut up! You yella bastard," Owen said between his teeth. "You a coward for not taking revenge that night and a coward if you don't want to find that gold. That's why we founded this town. That's why we built all of this! That blasted mine!"

"And soon it'll be a ghost town. Goldfield will be abandoned and ain't nobody gonna care about it. And I'm okay with that."

"I found it," Owen said again.

"Were your brains cooked in the sun? We ain't going-"

A gunshot rang throughout the building. Hiram coughed and felt his mouth swell with blood. He glared at Owen as he collapsed. Owen stood over his friend and watched the blood fill the cracks in the floorboards.

"I found it... I found the mine," he was almost confused why someone wouldn't want to go after it. As if the answer wasn't right in front of him. But Owen was too blind to see it. He only saw his goal and he was just as hellbent to get to it.

~

The old man, Jacob Waltz, worked up the trail again. His back so bent outta shape, that any incline brought him to a crawl. He didn't even need to bring a lantern anymore. He knew the trail by memory and knew every foothold and landmark. He knew the number of stacks on the mountain top. Least, he thought he did. Tonight, he had to stop and count.

"Prayin' Hands, the needle, crooked needle, Pointed Peak," Waltz mumbled to himself as he turned around and named all the geological features that guided his way. When he turned around, the rock stack he didn't recognize was gone. Waltz blinked and cursed his poor eyesight. The black night didn't help much either. "Might've been a cloud blocking the stars," he thought. He looked around and noticed there weren't a lot of stars out anyway. The whole sky might've been covered by thick dark clouds and no one would have noticed. "Storm's coming. Better get to cover."

Waltz hurried over his invisible trail to get inside the mine. Now, I don't know if mining underground during a thunderstorm is the wisest decision he ever made. But I guess he thought it was a better alternative to hiking back down and getting caught in a thunderstorm on the jagged slopes.

It had started raining by the time he had reached the entrance to the mine. If Jacob would've looked back over his shoulder like he did in town, he would have seen a person standing behind him. A bolt of lightning showed a man with one hand, standing in the rain glaring into the depth that Jacob disappeared into. With another flash of lightning, the man was gone. The deafening downpour making it all the easier to be followed.

Jacob followed the dark of the cave by the same muscle memory that took him up the trail. The deep parts of the cave were so twisted and crooked that a snake could break his back trying to follow it. Suppose the deeper into the earth it went, the closer it got to its maker. Even with the increasing amount of lightning coming from the outside, it was impossible to see past the first bend. If it weren't for Waltz lighting a lantern at his work sight, his pursuer would have never found him.

Owen saw a light appear in the deep abyss. He had no sense of where he should have been going and often lost the wall he was trying to follow. As soon as the dusty light radiated into the mine, the way became clear. There were no forks in the tunnel or dead ends, just the one way.

Jacob picked up his axe to put his first cut into the wall, when he heard a footstep. He immediately blew out the light and drew back into the darkness. A black silhouette came into his view. He might've have been able to see in the dark, but Waltz wasn't a sneaky man. Owen heard sharp breathing and could still see the ember burning on the wick. He knew his prey was close.

Jacob tightened his grip on his pick, his lungs hurt from trying to breath silently. A muzzle flash burned with the sound like a cannon. In the instant of the gunshot, both men had seen the other. But the bright light to blackness again took away either of their visions. Owen, with his left hand, cocked his pistol a second time. Waltz charged at the sound and hit Owen in the gut with the topside of his pickaxe. As Owen fell, he fired aimlessly. The bullet ricocheted off the ceiling and further down the cave. The flash of light again exposed both men. Jacob brought down his pick axe on where he'd seen Owen laying, but he only hit solid ground. He quickly swung around him, but the sharp pick only cut the air. Footsteps quickly fled the scene. Jacob pulled out his pistol as he followed. As the two men ran, the sound of rain became louder. Water flowed down into the cave like little rivers and turned the dry sand to mud. Owen kept bumping into walls as he was trying to escape. All he could do was fire back into the cave behind him and hope he could hit his enemy. Ten inches of flame came from his pistol with each shot. Jacob ducked as he heard each gunshot, hearing the bullets whiz and bounce off the walls.

Finally, they came to the edge of the mine. Owen ran out a few paces before turning back. Flashes of lightning overhead showed Jacob standing at the mouth of the mine. Each man had their pistol drawn and glared down the other. They exchanged no words. Jacob knew men would be after his mine and now, it happened. There was nothing personal. With the next flash of light, the men fired. The gunshots couldn't even be heard over the roaring thunder. With the next flash of lightning, Jacob saw that he hit his opponent. Holstering his pistol and adjusting his grip on his pick, Waltz walked over to Owen. The man was trembling with rage as he always had, but now he could do nothing about it. He was through. Jacob Waltz didn't care to let him die, he needed to do it himself. As soon as he reached Owen, Waltz swung and drove the pick into his skull. He left the pick and body as he quickly made his way down the mountain.

Waltz's Ranch

Jacob woke up coughing and spitting mucus. His bed was cold and wet, he supposed he'd fallen asleep before putting on dry clothes. He'd forgotten that his horse was left out when he went into the mine. He found it standing under a juniper tree, trying to stay dry. Surprisingly the horse wasn't as sick as he was. The old man hardly had the energy to get up and start a fire in his wood-burning furnace. He coughed up a storm as he tried to breath. He wrapped himself in whatever dry blankets he had left and pulled himself to his drawing desk.

Waltz took out an inkwell and parchment paper. He dipped his pen in the ink and went to write. With a fit of coughs, he realized he'd dripped ink all over the page.

"Son of a-" He grumbled before couching again. He dipped his pen again and wrote on the page all the same. After he was done, he waited for the ink to dry before folding it into an envelope. He knew there was no one to pick up letters from his house. He didn't even give the post office his location. Waltz hated going into town on any regular day, but he especially dreaded going out when he was sick. If he wasn't feeling his best, he couldn't as easily defend himself. He might even be seen as a weak old man.

Nevertheless, he threw on a pair of jeans over his long johns and wrapped himself a few layers of shirts and a heavy coat. He must've had a least three pairs of socks on, because his boots hardly fit on his feet. Jacob found his horse sleeping in its stall. It was old and grey and sickly looking.

"Come on," he pushed on its side to wake it up. It was laying down and was too exhausted to reach back and bite Jacob, though it wanted to. The horse snorted and laid its head down again. Waltz probably figured this would happen for constantly neglecting his horse. But he needed it all the same. "Come on, girl. I'll give ya a bath if you let me take you to town."

The horse continued to give attitude. Jacob went to the other side of the barn and brought back a whip. Immediately the horse shot up to its feet.

"That's what I thought," he said as he exchanged the whip in his hands for her saddle. He rode around the mountains to Goldfield. The horse slowed to a stop as soon as it stepped foot in town. Jacob knew it was too stubborn to go any further that day. He dismounted, keeping himself wrapped in his heavy jacket and coughing as he went along. He ignored everyone on the streets that morning and walked straight down the middle toward the post office. He passed through a crowd of people rushing to the bank. Behind him, the sheriff could be heard, "Get back! Everyone get back!" But Waltz was too focused to notice or even turn his head at the scene of a dead body being dragged out of the bank.

When he did reach the post office, Jacob merely slammed his hand on the counter and left behind an envelope addressed to Württemberg. Before the post man could object and say that sending a letter that far would cost a small fortune, Jacob pulled out an envelope of cash from one of mis many layers. He dropped the envelope onto the counter. The postman, wearing a thin visor, thumbed through the cash and took what was needed for postage. He put the rest back in the envelope and held it out to Jacob. Waltz snatched it and walked out the door without a single word.

The letter was taken by a coach heading East along the Butterfield Overland Mail Route. It went as far as the Mississippi River and all the way to the Pacific in the other direction. From the end of the line in St. Louis, the stage could take any number of trails up and over to New York. Along with thousands of letters and other goods to be sent over to Europe, Waltz's letter found its way onto a transatlantic steamship. It would remain in the cargo bays for 6 weeks before being unloaded in Britain. From there, the letter was sent across the channel and handed off to the Kingdom of Württemberg. The letter was eventually delivered to the homely farm. The large family gathered 'round to read this letter that had come from America.

To the Wisner Family of Württemberg and my sister.

From Uncle Waltz, residing in Goldfield, New Mexico Territory, U.S. of America.

I am writing to request the help of your eldest son, Jacob. I understand he's now probably a strong young man of 30? And I'm sure, a good help on your farm. I have a ranch myself and have fallen very ill. I need the help around here and some other matters. I'll send money back with him. Tell him to meet me in Goldfield.

Hope Ma is still well.

Uncle Waltz.

Waltz younger sister never understood why he left and never once gotten a letter from him since he moved away. "But if stubborn old Jacob was asking for help, it was probably serious," she thought (of course, in her own language). "And no one should be alone when they're dying. Everyone deserves to have family by them."

Quickly she packed Little Jake's trunk and sent him off. The journey was longer and just as arduous for a man to travel over from Europe. Jacob Wisner was about twenty-eight (and only three years old when Jacob Waltz left for America) and never traveled anywhere on his own. It would be considered a miracle by his family if he made it to the boats leaving Britain. Two months on a steamship followed by months traveling by train and carriage. Little Jake never let go of his trunk and his tickets. And if anyone asked if he needed help or if he was lost, he would just reply, "I'm going to see my uncle!" He had a smile on his face at all times and waved to just about everyone he saw. His hair was balding and unkept.

"I'm going to Goldfield, New Mexico Territory, in zee U. S. of A. My uncle lives zere. I'm going to see my uncle," he recited for each driver or conductor on his journey. They all gave him the same, "hmm very nice," that someone would give a toddler. It was already the next year when Little Jake reached Goldfield and Waltz had only started to recover from his pneumonia.

There were a few problems with Waltz calling on his nephew to meet him in town. No one in town knew who Waltz was or where he lived and Waltz, himself was almost never in town. When Little Jake arrived, he went into both saloons looking for his uncle. He even followed a wench by accident when she told him he looked lost. When she brought him upstairs and started undressing, Little Jake froze and ran out.

It was luck that the next morning Waltz would be making his run into town to deposit some ore to the Thomas's General Store. He rode by on his pale, sickly horse and wouldn't have even seen his nephew sitting in an alley if Little Jake didn't recognize his uncle instantly.

"Uncle Valtz!" He sprang to his feet and smiled to finally see the man he'd traveled around the world to see. Jacob Waltz blinked at the skinny man who looked like he'd slept out in the street.

"Little Jake?" The old man called back.

"Uncle Valtz! It is you!" Little Jake went to shake Waltz's hand. The old man was trying to shush his nephew, not wanting a lot of attention drawn to them or for people to hear his name.

"I vas on a boat for a long time. Zen I vas on a train for a long time and zen I was on a vagon for a long time and now I'm finally here!" He spoke fast. His smiled never left him.

"Okay, yeah," Waltz put his hands out to try and get the man to quiet down. He got off his horse and walked along with his nephew, without telling them where they were going. "You look kinda lanky, son. You done a lot of farm work with your mom?"

"*Guten Tag!*" Little Jake waved to the people they passed. Some men only gave them sideways glances, but a few people waved back. There wasn't a lot of friendliness going around back then.

"D'you hear me, boy? How much farm work have you done?"

"Vell ma and pa let me push zee plow, but—*Guten Tag!*—zey don't let me near zee horses."

"Why not?"

"Zey say I can't handle zee responsibilities. Oh, but they let me feed zee hogs!"

"You're a little *off*, aren't you boy?"

"Zat's what people say, but I think people all act a little off."

"Hmm. Alright," Waltz stopped outside the general store. "Tell you what. You can rest up here for a week or so, then I'll send you back to your mother. Pay her for your troubles."

"Vhy's zat?" Jake stopped.

"Well... you said it yourself, you can't work with horses and I need you to look after my horse here while I'm at work."

"I can learn. I'm good at learning zings."

Waltz grumbled under his breath, but didn't say another word. He took out the sacks of ore from his saddle bags and walked into the general store. Little Jake stood outside for a moment, not knowing what to do. Waltz came back out and dragged the man inside.

"Good morning, Mister-" Julia Thomas stopped short of saying Waltz's name when she saw there was someone with him.

"S'alright. He's with me," Waltz coughed as he walked up to the counter. "For the meantime."

"*Guten Tag!*" Little Jake waved as he entered the store; Julia returned the greeting. His head turned from all the different items inside. Jars and tools and canned goods lined the creaky shelves.

"D'you hire a hand?" Julia nodded towards Jake who was still looking around excitedly.

"Nope... Don't think anyone would hire him," Waltz said but Julia shook her head.

"Seems happy at least. More than what can be said about the rest of this town. You especially."

Waltz waved the comment off and turned his back to the counter. Julia finished measuring out the pieces of ore and withdrew the appropriate amount of cash from the till. Still selling for $16 an ounce, Waltz was making hundreds of dollars at a time. Waltz took his cash and stuffed it into his wallet as Julia took the ore into the back room.

"Come on," he grabbed Little Jake by the arm as they left Thomas's General Store.

The Trail

When Waltz got up the next morning, he was surprised to see that his nephew was nowhere in sight. The door to his adobe house was unlocked and opened slightly. Jacob grabbed a six-shooter from under his pillow. Cocked and loaded, the pistol led Waltz around the house. Nothing seemed out of place. Jacob sighed with relief. No one had robbed him. Waltz was just about to carry on his day, when he remembered why he woke up with such a stir. His nephew was missing.

Waltz threw on his jeans, yellowing-white shirt, and worn boots before heading outside. He kept his pistol in hand as he moved from the adobe house to the other repurposed adobe buildings on the ranch. He got to the chicken coop and saw that they were eating fresh seed. He looked out in the pasture and saw that the cows had water in one of their feeding troughs. Waltz squinted, confused. He couldn't remember the last time he'd tended to his animals.

"*Guten Morgen!*" Little Jake shouted from behind. Waltz nearly jumped out of his skin. "I got zee eggs and fed zee cows. Even fed zee horse! Zough ma says I shouldn't go near horses."

"I see," Waltz said, still processing and trying to understand what his nephew was saying. "You really did all that?"

"Yes sir!" He beamed. "I usually do zat back home. Back home everyone gets up a lot earlier. Zat's alright if you like to sleep, Uncle Valtz. I took care of it for ya. It was hard cause I didn't know vhere everything vas."

"You really do learn fast. Well, I... I guess we can cook up some eggs and get started on the day."

"Vhat else do we have to do?"

"Well. The ranch is kind of a side job. My real work is *much* more important."

"I hope it's not too much responsibility. Ma says I can't handle too many-"

"I think it'll be just enough responsibility for ya," they talked as they went back into the adobe house.

Waltz made steak and eggs and coffee for the two of them. Little Jake could eat for someone twice his size and Waltz thought he might have to butcher one of his cows to keep up. But they had plenty of eggs and had no issue cooking a few more. Though he ate a lot, Jake had better manners

"So, this job I need help with," Waltz started. "I have no doubt you can do it-"

"Great! I always vanted to vork a real job, Besides the farm zhat is-"

"Now just hang on," Waltz raised his voice. "It's real important work. But it's even more important that you don't go telling nobody."

"People don't know vhat you do?" Little Jake seemed confused.

"Exactly. And it's gonna stay that way."

"Vell, our family are farmers and everyone knows ve're farmers. And Mister Luther up zee road is a baker and everyone knows he's a baker. And-"

"Look. My job is a little more dangerous than that. I can't have people knowing what I do. Okay, boy?"

Little Jake didn't understand why, but he nodded and said "okay" all the same.

"Good. Now if you could saddle my horse, we'll be off soon."

"I don't know how to do zat. Ma says-"

"Your ma ain't here. Now go on and saddle my horse. I gotta get everything ready, yet."

Little Jake left the house and went to the stable. Waltz took a deep breath and enjoyed the silence for a moment before getting up. He scrubbed their tin dishes in a wash pan then left them in the dirty water. Waltz went to pack his bag. He had a few more torches with a canister of oil. He also grabbed a pickaxe for Little Jake to use. Waltz had always kept his tools up in the mine unless they needed replacing.

Jacob Waltz was just putting his gun belt on when he heard his horse bellow followed by a loud thud. Waltz buckled his belt and ran outside. His cream-pale horse stamped around the stables. Little Jake was on the ground, holding his head.

"I tried to remember how it goes on. I used zee blanket and everything." He groaned as Waltz worked to calm his horse down. Waltz hadn't even looked at the saddle.

"Well, you put it on backwards, but you got the right idea," Waltz unbuckled the saddle and flipped it around.

"You get kicked?" Waltz asked as he smoothed out the blanket on the horse's back and sinched the saddle the right way.

"No... I tried to get on zee horse, zen it bucked me off. I zink I'm okay."

"You tried to get on her? You got some nerve deep down in there," He peered over at him. "Surprised she still has the strength to throw someone off. Getting old and worn, aren't ya?"

Waltz patted his horse and stepped onto the stirrup to pull himself atop the sickly horse. She snorted and adjusted her stance, but she was still strong enough to carry a rider. "Maybe two," Waltz thought. He thought it was old age that was making her weak and couldn't have recognized it was his own negligence.

"Right, boy. Git on up," Waltz ordered without turning to look down at little Jake.

"Mm-mm," he shook his head and look at his feet.

"Boy..."

Little Jake took a deep breath and walked back over to the horse. He felt her side, rubbing her hair. The feeling with the rhythmic breathing calmed Jake down.

"Come on," Waltz stretched out his hand. "I'll pull you up."

Jake grabbed his hand and the back of the saddle. He jumped to swing his leg over, but the horse reared up under the weight. It gave a loud neigh and Jake was back on the ground.

"Easy," Waltz managed to stay on the saddle. "Let's try it again."

"No," Jake backed out of the cramped stables.

"We're losing daylight, come on."

"No!" Little Jake shouted loud enough to spook the horse. She shuffled where she stood. "Ma says I shouldn't go near zee horses! I should have listened. I should have listened to ma. I can't ride zee horse!"

"Alright, Christ!" Waltz raised his hands to try and get him to quiet down. "You can walk beside us then."

Waltz kicked his horse to start walking. Jake followed at a distance. "And grab that bag," Waltz pointed at his backpack, still on the ground by his house door. Jake ran to get it and the extra pickaxe, then scurried to catch up.

Though he ended up walking, Jake smiled a bit. He'd never touched a horse before and just then, he nearly saddled it correctly. There was a lot in the world that scared Jake, but he always found a way to overcome. Waltz might not have seen it that way. To the old man, Little Jake was scared of his own shadow and not capable of much. Unfortunately, a lot of people saw Jake this way. And he knew it. So, as quickly as he felt proud of himself, his mind was filled with the lie that he was incapable.

The two made their way down the trail, Waltz, up on the pale horse and Little Jake scampering behind. Jake noticed his uncle was coughing into his handkerchief quite a bit. They were long, painful bouts. Yet, Little Jake hadn't the courage to ask him if he was okay. He really didn't want to let his uncle down, but the anger that Waltz carried in everything he did made Jake feel like it was his fault.

"Uncle's mad at me. I'm messing up again," he thought over and over. "'You can't handle zee responsibilities...' 'You're a little off,'" He began muttering to himself, repeating the words spoken to him. "'You're a little off, aren't you?'"

"What's that?" Waltz turned back. But as soon as Waltz spoke up, Little Jake was too scared to speak. "Hmph."

They arrived at the landslide a little before noon. Waltz tied his horse to the same tree he always did. The bark was fraying from where the lead was always tied. Many had seen this horse along the trail and often gave her food or water, but no one ever saw who it belonged to.

Without a word, Waltz began to climb up the rockslide to the trail. Little Jake followed behind, the heavy backpack bowing him to the cliffside. By now, the old man knew which rocks were solid and which rocks to avoid. He shared none of this with his nephew, only annoyed that he wasn't getting up the hill faster.

"Come on," he barked when he reached the top. He scanned the hills around them, worried they might be seen if they took too much time on this stretch. Little Jake shook, not wanting to fail more than he already had. He rushed his way up and rocks beneath him started to slip out of place. "Jesus, careful!" Waltz's eyes widened when he saw the rocks began to collect others on their way down. He didn't want the whole cliff to slide more than it already had. But soon Little Jake was on the trail and the rocks he'd knocked loose were settled on the ground.

Waltz turned and started again without a word. Little Jake adjusted his pack and followed behind. Neither one of them spoke until they got to the small tunnel, where Jake audibly whimpered. Waltz look back to see him frozen with fear. The walls of the cave close. Too close.

"Come on," Waltz groaned and rolled his eyes. He disappeared into the tunnel, his body blocking the light coming in from the other side.

"You can't handle zee responsibilities," Jake mumbled to himself as he took a few steps closer, braving the obstacle ahead. "You can't handle zee responsibilities."

Jake felt the tunnel wall as he entered slowly. He side-stepped a little bit at a time. About halfway through he hit his head on the ceiling. Jerking back, he felt the rocks on his spine. The walls seemed to be closing around him. He moaned and covered his head with his hands. The ceiling was closing in, he could feel it. Jake bent himself in half and stumbled over. Before he his face would hit the ground, he was caught. Waltz caught him by the collar and dragged him out of the tunnel.

"Christ, kid. D'ya ever leave the house before?" Waltz asked. Jake looked down, ashamed he needed help. "Huh?" Waltz asked loudly. Jake had nothing to say or only briefly looked up at his uncle.

The old man coughed and kept going. The trail hugged the cliffside as it wound up to the flats. On top of the mountain now, they walked past all the usual landmarks. Though, to Little Jake, their trail seemed arbitrary. Waltz weaved between the needles and stacks until he got to the mine.

This time, Little Jake moved backwards at the sight of a cave. The walls might have been further apart, but the inside was solid black. So black, the daylight couldn't even penetrate it. He was grabbed by the arm as Waltz started to drag him inside.

"No!" He fell to the ground.

"Listen here you useless-"

"No! Please!"

"Enough!" Waltz pulled his nephew up to his feet and shook him. "You're going in that cave, you hear?"

Waltz's shouting stirred up some crows on the mountain. He watched them and realized if anyone else was up here, they could have heard him from a mile away. His attention snapped back to the young man in his vice grip.

"We're going in that cave," he said again between his teeth. Waltz saw how scared his nephew was and let go of him. Only then did Waltz feel any guilt. The old man went and picked up the backpack that had been left on the ground. "If it makes you feel better, you can hold the light," he said, but didn't look up at his nephew.

Valley of the Sun, 1891

The Wells & Fargo Company was about to make their usual deliver to Goldfield. The stagecoach had carried a discrete container with other letters and packages. The Wells & Fargo line ran from San Francisco all the way to St. Louis. Most mining towns relied on these wagons to exchange their ore for cash at the San Francisco banks. The distinct red wagons behind a whole team of horses were fast and easily recognizable on the roads. A highwayman could see them coming from a mile. But people also knew that these coaches were some of the most protected as well. Shotgun riders guarded the front and rear of the wagons. Only very rarely did a group of bandits manage to overtake one of these.

Coaches also came from the East, delivering mail that these immigrants sent to and from their home countries. They also sent news about the war and what was happening in Washington. No matter who you were, it was a dangerous road to be on. Wagons often braved Indian Territory, happened upon battlefields, and crossed hundreds of miles of unforgiving road. And if you were a mail carrier, you always had to turn around and do it all over again.

The railway had already breached the wild West, bringing in more immigrants and moving cargo across the continent. But the mail wagons were no less present. Railways couldn't make any detours or change course, wagons could.

Now, I said that only rarely did highwaymen ever take down one of these armed wagons. But that doesn't mean they were invincible. Over the rugged trail from Phoenix to Goldfield—through the Valley of the Sun—the red Wells & Fargo cart creaked and rocked over each bump. Their riders scanned the open desert, looking around boulders and peering into thickets. Their guns were loaded and cocked. The team of horses passed between a couple of stacks. The riders tensed up with anticipation. It was passes like these that ambushes were common. But there was no one. A sigh of relief came over the young riders.

It was now Spring of 1891 and this team had been riding since late the previous year. They just began to think that this delivery would go off without a hitch. Not even a shot had been taken at them. The Superstitions were in front of them and the open skies were behind them, bleeding with the setting sun. The trail they had been following ran along a dried tributary of the Salt River. The riverbed sat five or six feet below the ground and was smooth compared to the rest of the earth. Little ripples of sand promised hope that this land had once seen water.

The team of horses turned at the bend in the trail. They took it a bit too wide and the left wheels of the wagon slid off the trail and drove into the bank. As the wagon tipped, the left wheels snapped off and were crushed as the coach rolled over them. The horses snorted and howled as they were dragged from solid ground and turned over. They landed on top of each other as the Wells & Fargo wagon crashed on its side. One of the riders had fallen off when the wagon tipped and was now crushed. Everything except for the rider's head and one arm were buried below the shattered wagon.

The driver was working to get the horses free from their reins. They were tangled and impossible to untie with the horses still squirming. The rider took out his knife and cut the leather ties. Quickly the horses shot up and bolted away.

"God dammit," he said, not knowing if they would return after they calmed down.

"Help us, would ya?" The other three riders were grabbing pieces of timber and wedging them underneath the broken wagon. The fourth rider quickly scrambled in the sand to get his hands under the edge. He lifted up as the others pulled down on their wedges. The stagecoach began to lift off the ground. The man trapped under screamed more as the wreckage that pierced him was moved.

The riders pulled their comrade out from below. His legs were red with blood and disfigured. A piece of timber had jut into his thigh and other splinters stuck out from his gut. Quickly, one of the crew took their belt and sinched it around his leg above the spot where the broken off timber still stuck. The man screamed with anguish and began to kick. The others held him down, but as they did, they saw just how much blood had already seeped into sand.

"We're gonna pull this out, okay?" The young rider who tied the tourniquet try to tell the man, moaning and tossing his head around.

"It's not worth it," the other rider said quietly. He was tan-skinned, half Apache, and wore a green and yellow poncho.

"On three, okay?"

"It's not worth it!" Everyone silenced. "He's gonna bleed out in a few minutes. He's gone."

"He's right," The eldest rider said. "We have to track down the horses and get these lockboxes to Goldfield."

"We're goin' to let em die?" The young rider protested.

"That's the job," The old rider snapped. "Now dig through the wreck and find those chests. We get those out of here first, then we can come back for the letters."

After a few minutes, the tension left the air and the men worked to gather the lockboxes and the bags of mail. They dragged their comrade's body a few paces up the river, just out of sight. The other rider kicked the sand over to hide the blood that had stained the riverbed.

"No sign of the horses," The driver came back from running along the trail.

"Do we walk the money into town? If'n we follow the river we can get there, right? Or pretty damn near," The young rider suggested.

"How much did we have left? Ten, fifteen miles?" The older rider asked.

The other rider sat without answer.

"Or do we build a fire and start in the morning?" The young rider asked, trying to get any sort of plan in place.

"You sure you didn't see those horses?" The other rider asked.

"Yes, I'm sure," the driver replied.

"Okay, we'll hike to town in the morrow. Get some help," the other rider suggested.

"We're still sitting ducks," The old rider spat on the ground. "We gotta be smart."

They put together a small fire as they discussed how they would go about hiding the money and getting safely to town.

The small orange flame bounced off the wagon, laying on its side at the bottom of the riverbed. They sat around, their guns always in reach. The sky was navy blue at this point and the sounds of night began to surround them. Crickets and distant howls. One of the men even thought they heard the "whooping" of Indians. They looked up and around, only imaging what dangers could be right above them. Bandits or coyotes could descend upon them at any moment. Or so the young rider thought. The older rider seemed calm. Years in the desert taught him that he couldn't worry about what *could* come.

~

In a small tavern called the *Cholla Corral*, a bit West out of town, Paul and his Varmints gang were smoking and playing cards. Their table was outside, under the canopy.

"Heard Sheriff's teaming up with Bill. Seen em together a few times. Even heard we might be getting a deputy."

"What of it?" Paul asked as he tapped his cigarette over the ashtray.

"Maybe they're preparing to bring us down."

"Bullshit," said Berns, one of Paul's men. He was a cheater and thief, who often stole from his own company. But never from Paul. He was thin with a cunning charm to him. "We all know Durant's got no deputy. And Bill's too stubborn to accept any official position. There's no reason they'd be after us."

"No reason?" Paul raised his brow. "If'n they have no reason against us, then we ain't doing our jobs. Or have we gotten lazy in the big town? It's civilized men like Durant that locked us away on Hell on a Mountain."

"Didn't mean it like that," Berns looked away.

"Don't matter what you *meant*. It's true. They should be afraid of us and what are we doing? Sitting here playing the same cards they do, drinking the same bourbon. He thinks he's in control of this town," Paul said grimly.

"So, what do we do?" One of the Varmints asked. "The people here are afraid of us, but if Sheriff's not, we ought to step it up."

Paul sat for a moment. He was content with the setup he had going. No one messed with him or his men, they got plenty of money from robbing people on the road or making raw deals with folk in town. But his was beginning to realize they *were* relaxing too much from their initial zeal against justice. He needed to prove that law has no reign here. He needed to make this town anarchy; he needed a wildfire.

Out of the silence, one of Paul's men spoke.

"D'ya hear there's a band coming to town Monday called the Varmints? Saw their poster up in town."

"A band?"

"Like guitars and-"

"I know what a band is!" The other outlaw shot back. Paul shook his head and sat out from their conversation.

"Just saying. Maybe we could get one of their posters. Have something with our name on it," The first outlaw spoke.

"We could show em who the real Varmints are," the other finished his drink and stood to get another.

Paul handed him his empty glass when he saw four horses galloping down the trail. They had reins around their heads, but they weren't tethered to anything. They watched as the horses slowed down, but kept going past their roadside tavern.

"Whatcha think that was?" Berns asked.

"Unless they were pulling a ghost wagon... I'd say they're a coach team that was cut loose."

"Why would someone cut their horses loose? And not even take off their reins?" Another of his gang asked.

"There's a wreck out there," Paul said, peering into the starless night. He blew a puff of smoke then got up from his chair. "We'll ride out before light tomorrow. See if we can't lend them a hand."

~

As the sun was rising over the bank of the river, the men inside still slept. The stagecoach driver was still leaning back against the wagon. The young rider found himself too tired to stay up worrying all night and lay relaxed in the sand. His gun not even near him. Not even the old, experienced shotgun rider was awake.

Upstream—if there would have been water in the riverbed—Paul and his men were crouched. From atop their horses, they were able to spot the wagon a few hundred feet from them. Now, they had dismounted and began to sneak the rest of the way. One at a time, the bandits went down into the river, where the sand would be quieter to walk on than the gravel trail. They all had their guns drawn and pointed forward as they followed the soft bends of the dead river. Paul stopped his slow approach when he came across a body. It was bloodied from the waist down and drained of all color. A small trench in the sand showed that it was dragged here from around the next corner. As Berns slowly craned his neck, he was able to see a wagon wheel sticking up from the bank. He put his finger over his mouth then pointed straight ahead to indicate they had reached their prey. Paul held up three fingers. Then two. Then one.

"Fine morning, gentlemen!" He stepped out from around the corner with his dual pistols drawn. Ten guns more behind him. The coach riders jolted awake. The old man reached for his shotgun, but Paul cleared his throat as he cocked the hammers on both his pistols. The old man slowly pulled his hand back.

"Now," Paul continued. "Last night a couple of horses came to us. Figured they was cut loose from a wagon somewhere down the trail. And no way anyone would tread these lands by foot. Not at night no less. That means only one thing. You boys have nowhere to go."

"We'll give you what we have if you let us live," The young rider interrupted. His hands were well above his head and he was sweating like a dog.

"Hell, what kind of bargain is that? We're going to take what you have even after we kill you," Berns snickered.

"But you don't know where we buried it," The old man spat on the ground.

"Buried *what*?" Paul squinted.

"The lockbox. Payment from the last gold shipment."

"Ain't hardly any gold in town. E'rybody knows that," Berns replied.

"Fine. If you don't think it's worth it to dig up a few thousand dollars... I'm sure the rattlers will find good use for it."

"How much d'you say?" Paul lowered his guns.

"Just over three grand, but the outgoing gold had a note that said a lot more would be on the way. Now you kill us," The old rider thought quickly, "You kill us and all that potential money slips away. Not a dime of it will pass out of this town if they know their shipment was hit."

"Theys taking us for fools!" One of the Varmints shouted.

"Not at all. I show you where we buried the box. Inside are notes saying whose money's whose."

"Why would we care about that?" Paul raised his pistols again. "It'll all be ours anyway. Stop messing around!"

"Now I can see that you gentlemen are reasonable, so, I'll continue," The old man was genuinely nervous. "If you knew who sent out thousands of dollars' worth of gold, they could lead you all to the *source*."

"You think we're going to mine for our money? That's what lowlifes like you are for. We're to take whatever you working men make for ourselves!" Berns interjected.

"You do whatever you want with that information. A wise man would see how valuable it is."

Paul gave no expression as he thought. Beads of sweat went down his scarred face. He hadn't really understood the exchange, but he didn't want to seem a fool. He understood one thing though, if they killed the men, they would never find the lockbox if it was real. He chuckled as he holstered his guns on the belt he once took off his old prison warden.

"Alright boys," he finally said. "Sounds like a fine deal. Now, you just show us where you buried that lockbox and we'll all walk away. No one gets hurt."

"Do I have your word?" The old rider extended his hand to shake.

"Of course," Paul smirked as he grasped the man's hand.

"Now could your men put their guns away?" He asked.

"No," Paul replied, still smirking. "You can still walk with them out."

The old rider knew there was nothing he could do. He grabbed the young rider by the arm, and in his other hand, grabbed the shovel. Then they started off down the riverbed. Paul and his gang followed close behind. The wagon driver was led with them at gunpoint.

"Where did we bury the chest?" The young rider asked quietly.

"Just up ahead," The old rider said between his teeth and tightened his vice grip on the young rider. "I don't trust these people, be ready for anything."

"Is there a problem?" Berns yelled from behind. Neither rider said a word. Eventually they stopped when they reached a rock in the middle of the riverbed. It was the same yellow stone as the rest of the earth around it. The old rider knelt down beside it and strained as he rolled the rock over. He took the shovel from the young rider and dug maybe two or three strokes before he hit a solid box. He knelt down again and reached for the metal handle on the side of the chest, which had been buried sideways. The Varmints peered around as he pulled the steel box from the earth.

"One lockbox, as promised," The old man handed it to Paul, who immediately handed it off to Berns.

"And the key?" He said, seeing the heavy lock still on the box.

"Let my guys go and I'll tell you where it is," The old rider said calmly.

Paul pulled his pistol out once more and held the end of the barrel only inches from the old rider.

"Just give it to him!" The young rider blurted out. Cocked the hammer of his gun.

"A wise man would see how valuable that is," Paul said coolly. The old man relented and dug in his shirt pocket for the iron key. Paul grabbed the key and put it in his jeans pocket. "A pleasure," he said then fired his pistol. Several more shots echoed out of the riverbed.

Sheriff's Office

Durant hummed to himself as he cooked breakfast that morning. His coffee steamed in the cold morning. Pancakes turned golden brown as he flipped them on his iron skillet. Light was just coming over the horizon and reaching through the shades of his house. If anyone else in town was awake, they were too few and far between to disrupt the peaceful silence. Like most men in town, he lived alone. He had a wife and family back in Mississippi, but decided not to take them when he took the job of a lawman in such a hostile town.

So, he ate alone and the burdens of this town seemed to weigh on him, having no one to share them with. It wasn't his fault that people didn't take a liking to him. He was the law in the midst of hundreds who had spent their lives escaping the law. Though Durant didn't care if people liked him or not, his primary concern was always that Goldfield stayed in one piece. As long as men weren't fighting and killing each other, he considered it a job well done.

He set his plate on the floor and let his dog finish what he'd left. Durant took a swig of his coffee, then walked out of the kitchen. From his wardrobe, Durant pulled out a jean shirt, put it on, and tucked it into his pants. Around his waist, he secured his holster and slipped in a Smith & Wesson revolver. Heading for his door, he put on a light duster coat, which had a six-pointed star pinned upon the left breast. Lastly, he put on his cowboy hat and left.

As he walked down the road, the Sheriff's Office could be seen. Already someone was waiting outside the door. Durant was in no rush and took his time getting there. The spurs on his boots chimed a little with each step. As he got closer, he still couldn't recognize who it was. "He looked to be Indian, but yet again, he's wearing normal clothes," Durant thought to himself.

"You the sheriff?" The man asked. His green and yellow poncho was covered in sand and his face was red and scratched. Durant had just now noticed he was picking cactus needles out of his arm.

"Christ, what happened to you?" Durant asked as he unlocked his office door and headed inside.

"Apart from running into a jumping cholla...? My name's Simon. I'm with the Wells & Fargo company. Our stagecoach tipped over outside of town. Our horses got loose and-"

"I'm not a charity. Get your own men to clean up your mess." Durant sat down at his desk.

"Look-"

"Sheriff, you gonna let me out?" An inmate called from the single holding cell. Durant forgot he'd locked someone up for the night.

"Hold on," he waved.

"Please, would you listen?" Simon insisted. Durant was listening as he was going over to unlock the inmate. "Our wagon tipped last night and one of our men died. Now, I went on ahead to call you in case the rest of my crew didn't show up. Seeing that they haven't, I think they was robbed."

Durant paused.

"Suppose it could be worth checking out," he set the jail keys down and went to pick up his coat again. "How far out of town d'you say you guys were?"

"Maybe five miles," Simon, the rider replied. "There was a helluva lot of cash there."

"And you didn't think to bring it with you here?" Durant turned to the rider, still holding the keys in his hand.

"It was a risk for me to carry it at night, same as leaving it with them. They had guns and all. Seemed best at the time."

"Fair enough. Mind if this fella borrows your horse?" Sheriff Durant asked the inmate as they were already out the door. They took the two horses hitched outside the sheriff's office and started up the road.

~

Jacob Waltz and his nephew had spent the last few weeks going up and down the mountain, making constant trips into the mine. They dug deeper each day to find where the ore vein had left off from the day before. So far as Waltz could tell, there was no end. The black depth seemed to go on forever. No one dared venture to see just how far it went. Not any of the Peraltas, not Waltz, and certainly not Little Jake who had major claustrophobia. They would all simply walk to where the gold stuck out from the wall and start digging. Neither Waltz nor the previous owner were scared by the abyss around the corner. The prize they dug out was a hopeful sign that the cave they were in was 'good.' A dangerous assumption to make when you are a few hundred feet underground.

Some days, Waltz would leave his nephew behind to take care of the animals, but sometimes he would take him with. The old man's back was starting to break from all the labor and needed someone else to swing a pick every once in a while. He caught on quick. Knowing when to swing a pick and when to use the smaller tools.

Waltz had spent so much time in the cave that he started to develop the same syndrome Miguel Peralta had, never knowing what time of day it was. Sometimes he would retreat from the mine at dusk. Other times, Waltz found himself exposed by the noon sun. He would come out of the mine, see the town below, and realize he could be seen if he weren't careful.

He forgot to take care of himself. His white beard was mangled and dirty. The rings around his eyes added to the look of constant paranoia. He forgot to bathe or brush off his teeth, which were stained and crooked.

He suffered for his determination, feeling the pain of hunger and thirst and exhaustion. In the mine, he would be struck by all these at once and nearly collapse. But he didn't stop himself. Jacob would simply push himself upright again and keep swinging. If not for Little Jake asking about food at regular intervals, Waltz would have starved.

This time, when he finally called it quits, it was dawn. The faint lights from town below flickered orange and yellow against the black skies, slowly filling with color. This time around, he'd left his nephew at home. Waltz walked back down the trail, his back aching under the weight of gold slung over his shoulder. The ore bits pressed into his spine and made every step hurt just a little more than the last. By the time he got down the trail, he jumped when he saw his horse, pale and hungry. Still standing where he left it.

"Almost forgot about you," Jacob patted the horse on its neck. He loaded his bags unto her back and lifted himself onto the saddle. He scanned the desert around him, making sure no one else had seen him. There was nothing awake but him and the multitude of crickets that chirped in the bush.

Jacob clicked his tongue to queue his horse to start walking. It was slow, and even more dehydrated than Waltz. Now that he was out of the mine, he realized just how tired really was. They eased their way back to the ranch. As he came around the bend, him and his horse were both spooked to see eleven riders darting past them on fresh horses of their own. They were cheering with crooked laughs and firing their guns in the air.

"Out of the way, oldy!" They flew past him. Waltz' horse kicked and snorted at the commotion. But the Varmints passed by him soon enough.

"Damn ruffians," Jacob spat on the ground.

As Durant and Simon turned out of town, they saw in front of them, about a dozen riders taking the trail that cut between Goldfield and the mountain. Durant recognized them right away and pulled back on the reins to stop his horse.

"What?" Simon looked between Sheriff and the posse that now rode into the distance. "Was that them?" He leaned forward, ready to chase had he been given the word.

"Show me where your wagon tipped. We'll deal with them later."

"But they'll get away!"

"Their camp is about three miles down that road. You want to take on twenty-five ruthless killers, be my guest," Durant waited until Simon was calm before speaking again. "They ain't going nowhere. Now, if you have all the ledgers and know exactly how much they stole, we can work on getting that back later."

"Alright," Simon kicked his horse, not taking his eye off the group of riders. They continued out of town and West on the trail toward Phoenix. Simon retraced the windy road that he took that last night. Not far into their ride, the two men saw the underside of the heavy stagecoach sticking up from the dried riverbed. As they drew closer from atop the trail, Durant could look down and see the crushed wagon wheels and splinted red walls. Letters were scattered and softly mixed with the sand in the wind. The sacks of mail were cut open and emptied by the Varmints rather than a result of the crash. Durant pulled his horse to a stop when he looked straight down and saw the dead rider, who had bled out overnight. He sat against the slope of the riverbed, his jeans were soak-filled with blood, now dried in the sun.

"He was crushed when the wagon fell. Didn't have a chance of making it," Simon said as he got off his horse. The two slid down the slope of the river and walked around the wreckage. Simon picked through the mail sacks, seeing what of their deliveries had been lost. The bandits didn't bother with the letters much, seeing there was no money or jewels in the envelopes.

"Where's the rest of your crew?" Durant asked, looking around and seeing no other bodies. Simon had realized he hadn't seen anybody either. Without a word, he walked up the riverbend. Durant followed behind. They didn't have to walk far before they found three bodies. Each of them dotted with several bullet holes, filling the sands with red blood. The old rider was face-down, with a hole straight through the back of his head.

"I'm sorry," The sheriff finally said.

"I didn't know em. Not that well at least," Simon shrugged. "Been taking odd jobs around Phoenix for a few years. They came through needing a hand."

"You didn't make it very far."

Simon chuckled.

"No, this wasn't my first time passing through. Gone this route three... three and a half times."

They studied the sight a little longer, seeing the men's pockets had been emptied and their rings and wallets had been taken from them. Simon knelt down next to the old rider and, turning him over, reached into his coat pocket. He pulled some tri-folded pieces of paper. Blood had only stained the top edge of the beige parchment. Simon stood and handed the papers to Durant.

"What's this?"

"Ledgers. How much money and who it was being delivered to."

Durant unfolded the papers and looked them over. Most of the money being sent to Goldfield was going to the two big stores, the goldsmith and Thomas's General. Durant's eyes widened when he saw how much money was going to Thomas's.

"Yeah, they stole a lot of money."

"It's not that," Durant folded the papers and put them into his own duster coat. "It's who the money was being sent to."

"What do you mean?" Simon followed as Durant had turned back to walk to their horses.

"Thomas's General Store. It's damn near out of business. No one, and I mean no one, exchanges their gold there. Why they were getting more than three times the cash our goldsmith was getting, is beyond me."

"Would that matter? I mean, to get the money back?"

Durant scrambled up the slope of the river and mounted his horse.

"Maybe not. But we might have just discovered something big."

Varmint's Camp

On the East side of Superstition Mountain, at the bottom of an alcove in the rock face, sat the Varmint's camp. The bandits were still celebrating their recent hull, whooping and cheering as they got in, bragging to the men who had missed the opportunity. Paul withdrew away from his rowdy gang to his adobe. In his hand was a folded piece of paper. On it, written roughly in charcoal, were the names and dollar amounts of who the money was being sent to. Berns was sitting at a table not far from the cave where the adobe had been built. He was splitting up the cash for each man who'd been a part of the robbery. For every few dollars that he gave to the crew, he would slip an extra for himself.

"Get your cut, boss," Berns called back to Paul, who was still murmuring to himself.

"The source," he said softly, eyeing over the paper.

"Boss," Berns said again. This time, his boss snapped out of his thoughts and went over to collect his stack of cash. Men were still standing around, counting the cash for the sake of feeling money between their fingers.

"How come I only got two hundred an' forty-five, when Billy got two fifty-one?" One of the men, Leroy, protested.

"We all know you can't count for shit," Berns called back. The men around him laughed as they slowly left and went about their own business. Leroy left, confused, but without another word. Paul only flipped the cash with his thumb before tucking it away in his wallet. Instead of going back into his house, he unhitched his horse and started to walk it out of camp.

"Where you going?" Berns followed behind on foot.

"You have to be a dog at my heel?" He got on his horse and rode out of camp.

Paul rode alone along the foot of the mountain and eventually veered off to go into town. He slowed his horse to a slow walk. People on the streets knew to move out of the way. But he wasn't out to intimidate the townsfolk right now. Over his left shoulder was Thomas's General Store. Ahead and to the right was La Taberna. He stirred his horse and hitched it outside the saloon. He looked around him once more before entering the dim saloon. It was around noontime and the place had just started to take in customers.

"Mr. Paul," Roberto, the man behind the counter, greeted with some nervousness in his voice. Paul Harris was easily recognizable by the large scare on his forehead and the mean look he carried with him. Without needing an order from the bandit leader, the bartender took out a bottle of whiskey and a glass. Those inside the saloon also got quiet when they saw the man walk in with such determination. This wasn't his usual place, but his reputation was known all the same. If a killer walks into anywhere with that much purpose in his step, it was almost certain someone was going to die. The room held its breath as Paul went to the counter. He grabbed the bottle and glass and turned to go up the stairs on the other side of the tavern.

"Send up some food," Paul said without turning back to the bartender. He walked up the creaky stairs and headed for the front windows. He found a table in the corner where he set down his glass and bottle.

"Git," he said to the man who was already sitting there. Without question the man fled. Paul pulled the chair to the far side of the table, with its back against the wall. From this view, Paul could look back down the road and see Thomas's General Store. He set his hat down on the table, pulled the cork from the bottle, and poured himself a glass. He'd been on stakeouts before and he certainly knew patience when he needed it. That was his key to surviving: know when to wait and when to strike.

And wait he did.

Eventually, the bartender brought up a dish with stew and a fresh loaf of bread. Paul ate and drank at a slow pace, always watching out the dirty window, keeping his gaze fixed on the general store. To his notice, it wasn't a busy place.

"The mortician's office had more life in it," he thought. The streets were busy enough and people were going in and out of stores, but not this one. He wasn't in town enough to know the gossip about it being run by a colored woman, or that the woman was married to the previous store owner, Mr. Thomas. Soon, though, he picked up the same suspicion that the sheriff had. A store with no customers shouldn't have that large of a money order. Something was off. Something secret must have been happening. And now, he wanted to know what.

To his surprise, someone eventually opened the door. Two men disappeared from the bright streets into the dark interior. He didn't see who they were. The one was wearing a hat, hiding his face from this angle and the other, the darker man, he didn't recognize.

Of course, it was Sheriff Durant and Simon who had entered the dusty building. The two looked over the abandoned store. Everything was covered in dust, and even the air was filled with particles. Only a few wooden boxes and picks looked new. Durant let out a cough and fanned the air with his hat. Only then did they realize they were not alone. A dark woman stepped out from the back room with a broom in hand. She clenched the handle tight as if she was expecting to fight off trouble.

"Oh, Sheriff," Mrs. Thomas relaxed a bit. "You startled me is all."

"My apologies," Durant coughed again. "You mind putting that broom to use and cleaning this place up? It's filthy in here."

"No use no how," Mrs. Thomas set the broom down and walked up to the counter. "Not like anyone comes in. You all know that."

"Even so, it would seem business has been... good recently," he started.

"Does it look like business is *good*?"

"Looks, no," Durant continued. "No, most folk would walk in and think this store had belonged to a ghost town. But you were supposed to get a whole lot of gold money delivered here and by the looks of your newest stock, you've been trying to outfit miners."

"What of—wait—what do you by mean 'supposed to get delivered'?"

"I was on the mail coach that was carrying your money," Simon jumped in. "We were robbed last night by a group of bandits. Only I escaped, but all that money is gone. Well, not gone, but out of reach. From the ledger, it looks like you lost quite a bit."

"So, shouldn't you be out there trying to get his money?" Mrs. Thomas blurted.

"His?" Durant inquired.

"Dammit! I..." Mrs. Thomas stammered.

"So, all that money was going to one miner? Who?" Simon asked.

"I swore not to tell. He only comes here cause he doesn't want to be found out, ya see?"

"No one keeps a mine a secret," Durant shook his head. "That's what gets ya killed."

"This man does. Shit, and now he can't even get paid. He's gonna kill me."

"Who is it?" Durant pushed.

"I can't tell you. I... If he found out I told anybody, I'm gonna be dead ya hear?"

"If not him, then the bandits," Simon said. Then the room fell quiet.

"Whatchu mean?" Mrs. Thomas trembled. "They just got my cash. How could they know it was going here?"

"The Varmints rummaged through the ledgers," Durant spoke up. "Paul and his boys. They saw what money was going where. That's why we came. The suspiciously high amount of money going here makes you a target. Next time, they might not wait for the mail wagon to show up. Next time, they're just going to rob you."

"Well, what can you do? Can I get some sort of protection?"

"Sure. It's free to stay in the jail," Durant scoffed. "I don't know what more I can do than warn you. But if you told me who this money was going to, he could help us get it back."

"I can't tell. I mean, I could talk to him, but I can't tell ya boys now," Mrs. Thomas shook.

"Then you're on your own," Simon said as he turned to walk out. Durant followed behind. They pulled the door open and went into the bright world outside.

"You got quite the knack for this," Durant said as his eyes adjusted to the light.

"For what?"

"You held your own trying to get information from her. I'm impressed."

"Just think looking into this is the right thing to do," Simon replied.

"So, it is. Come on," Durant put his hat on and led Simon out into the street.

From the window of La Taberna, Paul studied the men that walked back into the street. The sheriff was escorting someone. It made sense to Paul. If someone was supposed to pick up such a great amount of money, he'd have protection. Paul put his hat back on and went to leave.

He rode out from town quickly, trying to plan on the way back to his camp how to go about the situation.

"We'll start a watch in town," Paul addressed his gang that night. "There's an injun man that the sheriff's been guarding. He's our target."

"We're not going after the store anymore?" Berns asked.

"D'you hear what I said? We're going after someone else. He won't be hard to spot, but he *will* be with the sheriff. Them two went in and out of the general store. For sure he's our guy."

"Yessir," Some of his men got up from the food they were cooking and went to saddle their horses.

"But why are we after him now?" Berns followed Paul back to his adobe. "Wasn't stealing the money enough?"

"Getting real tired of you, boy," Paul snapped. "Sheriff's obviously guarding him. Means it was *his* money. Means, he's got more! Plus, if we take out the man Durant's trying to protect, this town will know who's in charge."

"I'll come with you, then. To kill him."

"You're staying here. I've had enough of you. Following me 'round like a lackey," Paul left Berns where he stood. Half a dozen men were already riding out of their camp to stake out around the town.

Thomas's General Store

Had Paul or even the sheriff waited just a bit longer, they might have seen two more men enter the square wooden store. One's back was crooked and his white hair kept under a large round hat. The other was skinny and nervously followed behind. Jacob Waltz wasn't inside for very long before his voice boomed to the outside.

"Stolen?!"

Julia Thomas tried to speak, but Waltz gave her no time.

"You lost me thousands! You hear me?! Thousands!" Jacob turned over one of the display shelves. Shovels clamored onto the floor. Mrs. Thomas gasped and shrunk back behind the counter.

"Uncle Valtz, vhy did you-" Little Jake began to ask.

"Quiet!" Waltz hollered without looking.

"It's not gone," Julia tried to assure him. "'It's just outta reach,' that's what the sheriff said. You could get it back."

"Get it back?" Waltz chuckled and shook his head. "How's a man supposed to do that!?"

"Sheriff knows who has it. But he can't try and take it back himself. He needs help."

"Uncle Valtz..." Jake tried to interject, but no one paid him any mind.

"I ain't helping nobody get back the money I already worked for!"

"I'm sorry! It's not my fault. The carriage was robbed before they even got into town!"

Waltz had turned around, not standing to look at Mrs. Thomas, shaking his head at her pleas.

"And I'm guessing you told them whose money it was?" Waltz turned back to face her.

"No, I swear! They have no idea."

"You're sure?" He leaned over the counter she was cowering behind.

"Yes, I swear!"

"You better start packing this place up. Ain't no way I'm trusting you with my money again!"

"Valtz..."

"Everyone got robbed! Can'tchu hear? The wagon with everyone's money was robbed. But now they're coming after me because we had the most money out of anyone and they think I'll have more. I've already given you all I have as it is."

"We?" He scoffed.

"Fine. They're coming after me now because *you* had the most money. Jesus, what does it matter? They're going to kill me if they don't get what they want!"

"You're lucky I haven't killed ya myself," Waltz was starting to calm down, realizing it wasn't Julia's fault.

"Uncle Valtz, why did you push zee self over?" Jake finally asked in the silence. Waltz sighed and only looked up at his nephew.

"The sheriff knows where it is, you say?" The old man continued.

"Yes... Him that his deputy said they knew. I can tell them I hired you to get it back for me. Please. If you help them, you can get it all back. Plus, if you take care of them now, they won't come after me."

Jacob squinted, thinking about his options. He grumbled to himself as he realized he either had to let all that money go or work with others to get it back. He didn't like either one, but he'd be damned if he let all that money go. He stooped down and put the shelf back in its place. He opened his mouth to apologize, but instead said,

"I'll talk to the sheriff," and stepped over the shovels on the floor and hurried outside.

It occurred to Jacob Waltz he didn't know where the sheriff's office was. He hadn't been inside most buildings in town, nor really cared to read the signs that hung over their doors. There was the bank, but he kept his cash—well I don't exactly know where he kept it, being so paranoid—but not in the bank, that's for damn sure. And there was the doctor's office, but letting another man take care of him was too invasive in Jacob's mind. And certainly, he had no need for a sheriff. He could protect himself, Waltz made sure of that. Nevertheless, he found the white adobe office with a wooden star hanging off its roof.

"Why don't you go on back home?" He said to Little Jake.

"Vhy? Vhat's going on?" Jake was too distressed in the store to follow why his uncle was so upset.

"I got some things to do, I need ya to go back to the ranch and take care of the animals."

"I can help. You know I can!"

"Not this time. I need you to go home."

"I-I don't know zee vay."

"Sure, you do. It's out of town. Just-" He hesitated giving directions to his house aloud. "Just follow the trail."

"I can't," Jake protested, starting to get riled up. "I can't!"

"Okay. Okay," Waltz hushed him. "Just stay in town then. Buy yourself a drink. I'll be back for you."

Waltz fished out a few dollar bills from his wallet and gave them to Little Jake. He said he'd meet Jake at the Cantina, then shooed him away. Only then did he realize the door was locked and the sheriff wasn't inside. He quickly turned and caught up with Jake.

Paul Harris was outside in an alley; his eyes fixed on the sheriff's office.

"No sign of the Indian," another man came up from behind the buildings. He saw that Paul didn't move his gaze. "Is he in there?"

"No... and neither is the sheriff. A few more men came and went, but no one else," Paul shook his head softly at white adobe building. His cowboy hat shaded his face.

"Can't we just shoot holes in the water tower or somethin'? Why'd we have to get *this* guy?" The bandit asked.

"Does nobody listen?" Paul asked himself and kept a patient watch on the office. "Just keep going around to everybody and let me know once he's been spotted. Don't make a move until I get there."

The bandit shuffled away, kicking up some sand as he did. Paul knew he was outgrowing his gang. They seemed mindless to him. Each man just wanted to take whatever he wanted, but Paul liked taking his time. If he was going to strike, he wanted to have everything covered.

~

Waltz and Little jake were sitting inside the Cantina Roja. The old man wanted to go home immediately, but Little Jake showed signs of making a scene. So, Waltz choose the discomfort of being in public if it meant they didn't have attention drawn to them.

They sat at the far end of the counter. Waltz insisted on getting the seat next to the wall, so he could lookout over the whole room. He held up two fingers when the bartender looked their way. Soon, they were brought two pints of beer.

"You had much of this back home?" the old man asked his nephew.

"Hmm-mm," Jake hummed as he was taking a drink. Waltz couldn't tell if that was a *yes* or a *no*, but he didn't care to ask again. "Uncle Valtz?"

"*Shh*," he hushed. "What?"

"Oh! Sorry!"

"Keep your voice down for Chrissake."

Only when Waltz snapped did people even notice them. Little Jake flinched a little bit, but continued quietly.

"Could ve maybe take a day off?"

"Whatchu mean? *This* is time off, i'n't it?"

"Vell, yeah. But ve've been at zee mine for days now and I'm starting to hurt."

"You're starting to hurt?" Waltz took a gulp of his beer, then chuckled to himself. "How'd you think I feel all the time? Nothing but hurt all over."

"So, maybe ve can take a day off? I haven't had zee time to vork vith zee horse."

"No, you're done with the horse," Waltz shook his head.

"I vant to get better! I vant to learn. I'm good at learning things!"

"Okay. Alright," Waltz put his hands up to show Jake he needed to quiet down.

"Uncle Valtz. Vhy did you push zee shelf over?"

Waltz clenched his fist and tapped it a few times on the table, trying to restrict his annoyance.

"Because I was angry," he said between his teeth. "And if you keep asking me, I'm gonna push something else over."

"Okay. Sorry," Jake said. He felt the swelling of disappointment come over him again. He began muttering to himself. "You can't handle zee responsibilities. You can't-"

"Jesus," Waltz grunted and took another swig of his beer. He didn't have the capacity to tolerate any one. Least not someone who took more patience. In Waltz's mind, Jake should be able to just "straighten up" and learn to keep his voice down. It bothered him that it wasn't that simple.

"Stay here," he grumbled as he stood up. "And don't talk to no one."

With that, Waltz turned around and went for the back door. Once he was outside, he turned to the back wall, unzipped his jeans, and starting urinating on the ground. He sniffed and looked around. The next building over was the bank and Mayor's Office. Mayor Weathers was talking to someone in back when an appalled look came over his face.

"D'you mind?" Waltz grunted and shook his head. The mayor left, flabbergasted, and adjusted his vest and bowler cap as if he had become dirty.

Inside the Cantina, the older gentlemen behind the counter went to collect Jake's empty glass.

"Take it easy, fella," he smirked, seeing his small size.

"Okay!" Jake beamed. His pleasant temper piqued the bartender's interest. He stopped cleaning the counter for a minute and walked back over to Jake.

"Where you from? Don't sound like ya from around here."

"I'm from Vürttemberg!"

"Where?" The bartender broke into a laugh. "Ain't never heard of it."

"It's really far. It's across zee ocean."

"Suppose it is. Whatcha doing round here?"

"I'm here to vork for my uncle Valtz."

"That old man with you?"

Jake nodded.

"He don't vant me talking to strangers zough."

"I ain't a stranger, though, am I? I've seen you in here before. More than that old man. The name's Francis."

He was in truth about the same age as Waltz, but didn't look quiet as rough. He wore a nice vertical stripped button down, with sleeves rolled up, under a brown vest. He had a mustache, and if the company was good, even a smile.

"Jake. Zough everybody calls me Little Jake. Zat's because I vas named after my uncle Jacob. Don't vant people get confused."

"And what is it your uncle does?" Francis asked for sake of conversation.

"Vell, he's a miner up in zee mountain. But he doesn't vant me telling no body. He says I'm not supposed to talk to no one."

"Well, your secret's safe with me," Francis smiled, meaning it. Just then Waltz walked back in. His eyes narrowed on the man behind the counter.

"The hell did I tell you?" Waltz hit Jake on the back of the head. "Don't talk to no body."

"No, sir," Francis interjected. "I was just introducing myself."

"Plug it," Waltz snapped then turned back to his nephew. "Come on. We're leaving."

Waltz grabbed his hat and started out before Jake was on his feet.

From a few seats down the counter, one of the Varmint's, who was sitting alone, got up and followed them out.

Standoff in the Varmint's Camp

"We have to go for it," Simon said. They had gone back to Durant's house. The disadvantage to the gang not living in town was that they didn't know where the sheriff actually lived. So, while they had eyes and ears all over town, none of them knew his house was only down the corner from the main street.

"I told you 'No,'" Durant sat at the kitchen table, patting his dog who had its head in his lap. "They'd gun us down if we came charging in..."

"So, we don't charge, then."

"You want to sneak in?"

"If it means getting the money back. The longer we wait, the higher chance they'll have spent it."

Durant groaned, knowing he was probably right. Even if they had dispersed the money to their gang, there had to be *some* cash piled around their camp.

"When would we? They'll have guards at night and ain't no one can sneak in the middle of the day."

"They probably have guards no matter what. I'd say we wait until one or two in the morning. If they're the rowdy, drinking type, they'd be out by then, but not so rested they'd be sober."

"You sure you ain't done this before?"

"Snuck into a camp of bandits? No. I used to clean up for a saloon. So, I know when they'll be out."

"Fair enough," Durant said and stood. His dog whining at the sudden lack of attention. "There's probably a load of stolen goods in that rat's nest."

"We'll start with the money. We can't prove anything else."

"Right," Durant nodded. He realized now why so many sheriffs have deputies.

Sometime between the hours of one and two o'clock in the morning, Durant and Simon crawled over the ridge to peer down at the Varmint's camp. Though he knew of it, Durant had never seen the camp with his own eyes. He only knew what Bill told him of it. Simon, of course, knew even less. Now seeing it with their own eyes, it filled their expectations of being extremely difficult. Tents and wagons covered the valley below the cliffs. Smoldering fires and burnt-out lanterns gave them very little light to work with.

"Do you see anything?" Simon asked.

"Like a pile of cash just sitting out? No, haven't really noticed," Durant said as he looked through his binoculars. "It's probably in one of them tents."

"We can't search all of them."

"Nope. And I don't fancy we should split up either. If we find trouble, it'll be best if stick together."

"Agreed. We should check the tents in the middle, maybe work toward the back."

"Why so?"

"Well on the wagon, we kept the lockbox in the center. Underneath the bench. And at a bank-"

"Alright, I get it. Let's work our way down and see if we can even get that far. Keep your gun close," Durant said as he pushed up and began walking down and around the ridge. Simon followed close behind.

The Varmints camp was quiet. The two stopped behind some boulders before going in, but realized that no guards were out. There were barely any fires going and certainly no one was talking.

"I don't like this," Durant said.

"They're all passed out, I told ya."

"No," Durant grumbled. "Something else. Paul is too smart not to set a watch."

"Well, we can't speculate all night."

"You're right. On me," Durant said. He crouched low and held his pistol out. The two snuck up behind the first covered wagon. Durant was looking around for the next cover when Simon peered inside.

"This one's empty," he said quietly.

"Anything in it?" Durant looked back.

"Nothing that looks of value. Sleeping bag and some clothes is all."

"Alright, let's keep going..."

They lurched onward, looking all around them as they went deeper into the camp. At the center was a large tent with a dead fire outside. Tables and chairs stood around it. Durant looked in, saw there was someone sleeping inside, then quickly backed out. He shook his head and the two moved on. The man in the tent stirred.

"There," Simon whispered, pointing at the adobe house.

"We'll see," Durant said as they moved towards the cliff. The sheriff looked around more and realized how much of a bowl they were in. The cliffs surrounded their peripherals and the only way out was back through the camp.

"Let's hurry it up," he said when they reached the house.

"Locked," Simon pulled on the iron ring that was fastened to the door. Durant moved to see into the windows. A bed, but no one in it. A large chest and a reflection.

Durant turned around and cocked his pistol. Simon did the same.

"You managed to wake the one person left in camp," Berns said. His rifle pointing at the sheriff.

"Foolish thing to say you're outnumbered," Durant took his time to aim.

"That, or I'm giving ya a false sense of security. You fire, you could wake up fifteen men. Your wager, though."

"I'd take that bet," Simon raised his gun, too. Berns turned to him.

"Wouldn't be too sure. There's a lot of men out looking for you right now. Paul Harris wanted the special honor of killing you."

"Why?"

"You that stupid? He saw you and your bodyguard here going in and out of the general store. Bet your wallet's hurting, ain't it?"

"The hell you talking about?" Durant asked.

"Don't play games with me," Berns replied. "No one goes in that store."

"Which is exactly why we were there. We thought it just as suspicious that someone was making that kind of money."

"If you're not the miner, who are you?" Berns asked.

Just then a shot was fired. Leroy had woken up and staggered into the conversation.

Durant fired at him, while Simon aimed for Berns. The four each found cover.

"You idiot!" Berns yelled. Simon fired in the direction of his voice. The bullet shot through the barrel he was crouched behind and hit Berns in the collar bone.

Leroy advanced, firing round after round at the corner of the adobe house. After six shots, his gun clicked. Durant came out and shot him in the forehead.

"Told ya, you couldn't count for shit," Berns spat as he crept away. Simon and Durant spread out to look for him.

"There!" Durant fired at him as he saw his leg disappear behind a tent. As he rounded the corner, Berns was standing and clubbed Durant in the jaw. Before he could draw his gun again, Durant was back up and returned the blow, knocking Berns to the ground. Durant kicked his pistol away and put his knee on his bullet wound. Berns screamed in pain.

"Where's the money you stole?" Durant asked sternly.

"Like I'd tell you!" Berns spat at him. Durant put on more pressure. Berns tried to push him off, but his arms were going numb.

"Where is it?"

"*Argh!* Alright," Berns coughed. Blood was now filling his throat. "We divvied it out. It's spent."

"We'll take from your cache then. You have to have *some* money pooled up."

Berns only glared at him.

"Sheriff, we gotta go!" Simon called, hearing horses approaching.

Durant pulled out his six-gun and held it to Berns's nose.

"I'll ask you one last time, you sumbitch. Where're you keeping the money?" He felt a swelling in his head. He *needed* to know where it was. He needed to see that money.

Berns coughed as Durant pushed down on him again. He glanced over at one of the wagons.

"Let's go," Simon said again.

Durant pushed off Bern's chest and ran toward the wagon. He climbed inside and tore through the chests.

"Sheriff, we don't have time."

"Just wait!" he barked. He was starting to shake and sweat. Durant overturned the mattress and found hundreds of dollars spread out beneath. He started to grab handfuls and stuff them into his pockets.

"Durant!" Simon yelled and pointed. They could see Paul approaching.

Not a few seconds later, Paul's horse roared into camp. He swung off and stormed around to look for the intruders he was warned about.

"Find them!" He turned back and yelled at his men, still on their horses. They hurried off. Paul stormed around his camp until he found Berns, sitting up and trying to contain his bleeding. "Where are they?" Paul knelt down and shook him.

"They ran."

"They..." Paul stood up and walked in a small circle. "They ran?!" He turned and kicked Berns in the gut. He threw up almost instantly. "They took off with our money and you're still here?!"

Before Berns could defend himself, Paul had his pistol out and held it under his jaw.

"I didn't tell them anything," he begged.

"You left them alive... You told them they can fuck with us and get away with it!"

"I-"

"I outta kill you!" He screamed and held the barrel of his gun to Berns's head, but he didn't shoot.

"It's not the Indian."

"What?"

"It ain't him. He's not the source."

One of the men who had ridden back with Paul got off his horse and walked towards them.

"How do you know?" Paul's eyes narrowed.

"It's someone else," The other bandit said. "An old man and his nephew. They're Dutch. The kid's got a mouth on him and said more than he should've. Said something about them mining up in the mountain."

"And?"

"That's where the hidden mine is rumored to be," he continued. Paul looked back at Berns, who nodded along nervously.

"What was his name?"

~

"Sheriff!" Simon yelled once they were far enough away. The night was still black around them. "What the hell was that?"

"What?"

"You went crazy for a second. You just couldn't leave it."

"We needed to get the money back. We needed to get something."

"We were gonna get shot and you couldn't leave it. Don'tcha think maybe our lives are more valuable?"

Durant's mouth moved, but no words came out. Simon now gave him a different look.

"Hand over the money."

"Why?" Durant drew back.

"You want to keep it?" Simon squinted.

"No. I..." But Durant couldn't think of anything to say. He did want to keep it; he knew that for sure. He sat down, threw off his hat, and buried his head in his hands.

"We'll split it up tomorrow. Then it's out of our hands," Sheriff finally said.

"Okay," Simon nodded.

Goldfield Church

"Something wrong Sheriff?" the preacher asked as Durant walked in. After Sunday service, there were maybe a dozen people exiting under the small white steeple. Sunlight filled the light-colored interior. It wasn't dusty or full of sand like the rest of the buildings in town. It was clean and bright.

"Suppose you would think that being that I don't come in here often," Durant sat down on the back pew. Even these were light and looked like they were freshly sanded. Durant figured it was due to a lack of traffic in this building compared to most.

"We're not a godly town," the young preacher sat in the pew in front of him. He was still in his black suit with a white clerical around with throat.

"No, we ain't... It seems this town is full of bad men," said Durant. The preacher knew he was talking partially about himself. "It's all lawless."

"'Whoever commits sin also commits lawlessness, and sin is lawlessness.'" The preacher quoted.

"You come up with that?"

"First John chapter three," he replied. "Lawlessness leads to sin. That's why God gave us the Law. Without it, all of us would act like the worst of this town. The Law curbs our behavior, guides us to an ideal."

"So, what happens when a man falls from that ideal? What happens when a lawman falls from the Law?" Durant asked.

"You see our cemetery?" The preacher pointed out the thin, tall windows. "Most of the men in that yard were murdered. Ain't no one die of old age in Goldfield. Sickness and broken bones and a lot of bullets. Most all of them were after the same thing. And in the end, they got the same thing..."

"The grave."

"No," he said as though he hadn't thought of it like that. "A chance for grace. As bad as the men in this town are, there isn't one sin that ain't covered by the cross."

Durant nodded subtly, and swallowed the lump in his throat before standing and heading for the door.

"Sheriff," the preacher called after him. "Was there something you needed?"

"To hear your words might have been enough. But there is something on my mind. These evil things that are around us. It's our duty to get rid of them, is it not?"

The preacher thought carefully.

"We should abhor evil, yes. But we should also pursue what is good. As the man of the law in town, I'd say that is something you strive to live. Many people look down on places like this with contempt because they think the whole town wicked, but few strive to do what is good or even to acknowledge that there is forgiveness."

"Yeah... abhor evil," Durant repeated as he went for the door again.

"*And* pursue what is good," the preacher reminded.

"Hmm," he said simply.

"The men in that graveyard can't change the way they lived. But we can. We have a chance at grace."

"How?" Durant was at a loss. He'd been brought down to the same greed that fueled the rest of the town and someone was there to witness it.

"Stop running from it. Forgiveness and grace are there whether we realize it or not. All we have to do is believe it. From there, we start to strive for the Law, pursue what is good."

"Thank you," Durant put on his hat and left.

Durant walked down the street, passed the wooden water tower, and into his office. He opened and closed the door behind him. For a moment, the sheriff let out a sigh and leaned back against the door.

"You alright?" Simon asked from the desk, two stacks of cash lay in front of him.

"Never better," Durant rubbed his face as he pushed off from the door.

"I sorted out the cash. We'll take seventy-five percent to Mrs. Thomas and the other twenty-five to the goldsmith."

"Okay," the sheriff nodded as he poured himself another mug of coffee. He set the tin percolator back down on the small wood-burning stove. "And we're sure that's the way to do it? Goldsmith has more people to pay. We could slice it up so everyone gets the same amount."

"Thought of that," Simon looked down at the money he'd just sorted. "But if one man really dug up twenty-five hundred worth, he should be getting more than those who only dug up a few ounces."

"Okay," Durant agreed. "We'll drop them off. Let the goldsmith decide from there how to distribute it."

~

At Waltz's ranch, him and Jake were inside eating breakfast. The old man put Jake to work, while he was inside "thinking." Something had been bothering him about the other day. Something he heard. He just needed to be sure before he could make any decisions.

"Jake," Waltz said, it came out more sternly than he intended, hoping to at least sound like he wasn't furious. Little Jake looked up from his scrambled eggs. With a deep breath, Waltz continued. "Jake what were you talking about yesterday at the saloon?"

"I vanted to learn how to handle zee horse?"

"No. When you were talking to the man while I was outside. What were you telling him?" He spoke slowly.

"Zat I came over from Vürttemberg. To vork for you..." Jake began to realize where he'd messed up. "I didn't mean to tell him anything! Zee man was so nice to me! Vhy can't ve talk to people?" He began knocking his head in frustration.

"Did you tell him what we do?" Waltz was no longer trying to hide his anger. Jake didn't reply. Waltz stood and grabbed Jakes wrists. "Did you tell him what we do?"

"Yes!" Jake cried. Waltz let go of him and stepped away. "I didn't mean to! I... I messed up! I messed up! I can't handle... I can't handle zee responsibilities. I can't-"

Waltz fired his pistol. Jake fell to the table instantly. A look of madness was on his face. He breathed heavy, both in rage and in realization of what he'd just done. Before he'd been able to calm himself down when he went too far. Now, he was stuck on anger.

Waltz dragged his nephew out into the desert, his feet bumping along the rocks. Once he was out of sight of his house, he dropped the body and left it.

He felt like he could finally think clearly again. There was nothing now to distract him from his goal. Tomorrow he would worry about his stolen money. Tomorrow he would worry about loose ends in town. But today he would grab his pick and head up to the mine.

The Posse

The next day, Jacob Waltz rode back into town to seek out the sheriff. This time, there were lit candles and the door was partially open. Inside the sheriff's office, were too younger men. One was tall and blonde and wore a star. The other was part Indian, younger, and fiercer. They were talking when Jacob walked in and stopped short when they saw his grizzly appearance and wretched smell.

"What is it with people showing up looking rougher than hell?" Durant joked.

"I was told someone has to collect some money," Jacob said, not paying any mind to the humor.

"Talk to the smith, there's a lot of folk lost some money," Durant waved.

"Miss Thomas sent me... Told me you gentlemen needed help getting her money back," Waltz didn't let it show, but he was nervous walking into the sheriff's office after what happened yesterday. He knew there was no way anyone would find the body or know it was him, but Waltz was ever paranoid.

"You're her hired man?" Durant looked him up and down, seeing his crooked back matched the appearance of a lot of miners in town. "You seem like an unlikely candidate to be hired for such a job."

"I'm the man she asked. And though I don't ride like a colt anymore, still shoot *just fine*."

"We're not taking some eighty-year-old," Simon shook his head.

"You'll take the help you can git," Waltz grunted.

"Okay," Durant backed off, still not quite believing him. "We need to get one more man if we're gonna do this right."

"Another?" Jacob asked. "'Three's a crowd' they say."

"Three will seem mighty small when we face twenty-five," Simon said.

"Tw-Twenty-five?"

"That's right," Durant confirmed. "But if it's no personal interest to you, you can tell Mrs. Thomas to find someone else."

"I can handle it," Jacob grumbled.

"Good. Then you'll need to handle one more for the crew. Simon, get these wanted posters hung up. I need to find Bill."

Simon looked the stack of posters that had been printed.

WANTED

$$$ 5,000 $$$

REWARD

PAUL HARRIS

DEAD OR ALIVE

$500 REWARD FOR ANY OTHER
MEMBER OF THE NOTORIOUS
VARMINT'S GANG

Sheriff Durant put on his hat and left. He looked around quickly before shuffling across the street to La Taberna. Sheriff hoped Bill would just be outside, but the chair he smoked from was empty. Pushing opening the swinging double doors, Durant made his way inside. The piano in the corner played lightly. People inside were talking and laughing. It was hardly the rowdy crowd he had to break up across the street in the Cantina. Even after a short look around, Bill's big round hat was nowhere in sight.

"*Buenos días*, Sheriff," Roberto nodded. "Can I get you anything?"

"Bill."

"He's, uh, *el se está escondiendo*."

"In English, Roberto," Durant rolled his eyes. The man behind the counter waved for him to get closer. Then the Mexican man said in a hushed voice:

"He's in hiding..."

"Hiding?" Durant repeated.

"*Shhhh!*" Roberto begged. "He says the gang's watching. They're everywhere. These Varmints."

"What are they watching for?" Durant sat on the counter stool and asked quietly.

"They-"

"Hey, amigo! Another round," came from one of the tables.

"*Solo espera*," Roberto waved the man off. "They're watching out for you is what he said. You and that man you're with."

"So, where's Bill?"

"He said if you came asking... Oh, how'd he say it? 'The first building he'd been in.'"

"Okay," Durant scratched his head. "Thanks."

"Oi! Our drinks!" The man called again.

"Keep your head down, Sheriff," Roberto whispered as he grabbed another round of beers.

Durant took off once again, putting on his hat as he got outside and taking it off again as soon as he got inside the next building.

"Doctor?" Durant called. So far Dr. Thorne wasn't in sight and no one returned his call. Durant took out his six-gun and slid past the counter that separated the waiting lobby from the operating room. The curtains around the beds were all pulled shut. "Doctor Thorne, this is Sheriff Durant. You best come on out if you're in here."

"He's not here," A man stepped out from one of the curtains.

"Jesus Bill," Durant jumped and holstered his pistol. He realized Bill also had his weapon ready to fire. "The hell you doing here?"

"The Varmints are planning something big. They want to take us all down."

"I'm sure they do. They're outlaws, we're lawmen."

"I'm not just talking wanting to stick it to the system. They're scoping out the town and been watching your office nonstop. They're planning an assault."

"Why now?"

"Doesn't much matter. Heard something about a stranger sticking close by you, but no more than that."

"They seemed to think he was wealthy."

"How'd you figure?"

"We, well we snuck into their camp the other night."

"You have a death wish, Durant?"

"We were lucky that the whole gang was back here watching for us. But one of Paul's men seemed to think that this stranger, Simon, was the was the owner of their last haul. And seemed to think he had a lot more stored up somewhere."

"Guess it don't matter though. There's a fight coming and I can already tell why you came looking for me," Bill said.

"You in?"

"Who'd you think I am?" Bill asked as he pulled back the curtain around the bed he was hiding by. A few rifles, another shotgun, and a handful of pistols were laid out on the bed.

~

Paul sat in his adobe house, thinking over a cup of coffee. They could simply ride into town and shoot up the whole place. People already thought that was going to happen eventually. He'd heard of an outlaw gang that whipped out an entire town. But it wasn't long before all the marshals and rangers in the state mowed them down. He needed to bury Durant and anyone that stood with him, but he also wanted to stay alive. He almost wondered how Durant could bury himself.

Paul heard some of his men singing around the fire as they cooked. One of them had a guitar and another scratched the washboard he had. Then he had an idea.

"What day is it?" he asked himself.

~

Back in the sheriff's office, Bill was loading his pistols and double-barreled shotgun. There wasn't much noise other than the clicking of guns loading and the occasional bird whistling outside. Durant had introduced Bill and gave his credentials. He shook hands with Simon, who introduced himself, but Jacob only gave a nod. Still, none of them knew his name.

"We'll need more," Simon Tahoe shook his head. "There's another who could help us."

"We'll I'd love to hear about it..." Durant replied, thinking Shotgun Bill would be his ace in the hole.

"There's a rider. He's a nomad around the valley, but a fierce fighter."

"Chrissake, Simon," Durant took off his hat and scratched his head. "You, I can deal with, but ain't no *wild* Apache joining us."

"He's fought and won heavily outnumbered. He'll be an asset."

"How do we know he won't kill us?"

"I've heard a rumor-"

"A rumor?!" Jacob laughed. "I already didn't like getting more men, but this crosses the line."

"Twenty-five men, Sheriff. Not including their women who will also be shooting at us."

"He's right," Bill spoke up.

"God dammit," Durant cussed under his breath. "Well, who is this rider?"

"Delshay."

"Whatchu say?" Bill walked over to Simon.

"That's his name. Delshay. And the rumor was that-"

"Was that he was brought here to be treated by the doctor," Bill said. "Go, find him. We'll be held up here."

Simon looked to Durant for permission, who nodded reluctantly. Then, he left and took his horse outside of town.

"I hope you know what you're doing," Jacob scowled.

Being part Apache, Simon had always been drawn to the warrior of the valley. He heard stories of him stopping robberies and turning in bounties, but he was illusive as the wind. Simon doubted that anyone who had gone looking for him had ever found him.

Simon rode around the valley between Goldfield and Phoenix, going off the roads and following the more natural trails. He followed a small dried creek for a mile before he saw a think whisp of smoke. Simon rode towards it until he saw the buffalo skin tent it was rising out of. In front of the tent was a middle-aged man sitting with his eyes closed. He was shirtless, wearing buckskin pants and barefoot. Dried and cracked war pain was on his face. Yellow lines ran down his checks and a line of red ran across his eyes.

"Do you know how hard I tried not to be found?" Delshay spoke without opening his eyes.

"I need your help."

Delshay opened his eyes when he heard the voice of one of his own people. He was quickly saddened at his appearance.

"You cannot call on my help."

"There are a lot of bad men who need stopping and I heard rumors of a warrior living out here that stops bad men."

"That might be true. But I don't work for those who betrayed my people. You wear the clothes of a white man. Ride your horse like a white man."

"Well, you speak like a white man and live alone. I'm guessing you also betrayed our people. In one way or another."

Delshay closed his eyes and thought for a moment. Then he stood up and waved for Simon to enter his tent. A small fire was in the middle, the light flames were barely smoking.

"How do you know how to speak English?" Simon started out. Delshay pointed across the tent. Laying beside his sleeping mat was a copy of John C. Cremony's *Comprehensive Apache to English dictionary*.

"We met him in battle," Delshay spoke. "After we surrendered to his army, he became very interested in the Apache. But by then, I was already on my own."

"Is that when you came to Goldfield? To see the doctor?"
He nodded.

"My foot. It was filled with metal and a white man took me all the way to Goldfield. Saved my leg."

Simon noticed how one foot was scarred significantly.

"Why did you leave our people?"

"I didn't," Simon replied. "My mother was Apache and my father was white. She wanted him to raise me in 'civilization,' knowing I would be an outcast in our own. She didn't know just how outcast I was in white society though. I never met her."

"A lone wolf. Not belonging to any pack."

"Yeah," Simon sighed.

"You came to ask for my help."

"I did. There's a band of robbers, rapists, and murderers. They killed my crew and took all the money we were supposed to deliver. Now, me, the sheriff, and a few hired hands are going to take it back."

"So, why call on me?"

"Because this gang is twenty-five, maybe thirty strong." Delshay gave no expression.

"I've fought worse," he finally admitted. "I will ride with you. Give me some time to get ready."

~

Inside the sheriff's office, Bill had stolen glances out the bared windows.

"I haven't seen any of Paul's men," Bill noted casually.

"That's good right?" Jacob Waltz asked.

"They're been scouting the town for days. Now nothing. I don't think that's good," Bill replied.

"Like a snake retracting before the strike," Durant added.

"So, we're just sitting here until they come?" Waltz looked around. He'd been in gun fights. But only on his own against one or two others. Tactics and planning for whole teams were new to him.

"If we know they're riding in, we have to be ready," Durant said, adjusting his gun belt.

"Whatchu thinking? We hold up in some brick building and fire down on them?" Waltz asked.

"No. We take them head on. If we hold up in one of the buildings, there's a chance, a good chance, that they'll start shooting up the rest of the buildings. We don't want a massacre."

"Couldn't possibly go wrong," Waltz shook his head.

"Maybe we don't have to take them in town. We could draw them out. Ambush them on the road," Bill thought.

"I like that," Durant thought. "We could draw them toward the mountain. Hold up in the rocks. Either of you know the trails up that way?"

Bill had been around the mountain, but only on it once or twice. Waltz practically knew it by heart, but contemplated letting them know that. "It could be life or death," he thought.

"Yeah," Waltz finally grumbled.

"Good, we'll have you go up that way and find a spot for an ambush."

Soon, Simon returned with Delshay. Simon hitched his horse, but the Apache just told his horse to 'stay' and it did.

"How'd you do that?" Simon asked. "He listens to you?"

"Listens? No. Too stubborn to wander off."

The two made their way inside. Jacob and Durant both stood up and got stiff at the sight of the Apache dressed in warpaint, but Bill went to shake his hand.

"Good to see ya," he said.

"And you," Delshay replied and walked into the room, not knowing to shake his hand back.

"You two, uh, know each other?" Waltz asked, still drawn back against the wall.

"Yeah, we go way back," Bill said shortly, grabbing his guns. "Look, we don't have time for introductions. They're coming soon, if not, already here."

The posse loaded and holstered their guns. Bill wore a bandolier filled with both shotgun shells and bullets for his pistols. Simon tied his gun belt around his waist. Even Delshay cocked and loaded his lever-action rifle.

"You know how to use that?" Waltz asked. "I mean, you don't use a bow and arrow?"

The room went quiet.

"I only use bow and arrow if I want my enemy to die slowly. Plus, I like this much better. I once shot a man off his horse at a hundred yards with this gun."

"Oh," Waltz raised his brow. Simon chuckled and shook his head. "What?"

Goldfield Massacre

The five that made up the sheriff's posse left the white adobe office. Durant looked the part of the sheriff with his cowboy hat and bright star and spurs. Simon was right behind him, his dark hair hanging to his poncho. They both mounted their neat brown horses. Bill climbed up on his dark-haired horse and slid his extra guns into holsters on the saddle. They all looked twice when Waltz mounted his ride.

"You take the saddle off, that horse is gonna fall apart," Bill said, seeing the ribs on the cream-pale horse. Waltz didn't say anything in reply.

Finally, Delshay got on his horse, riding bareback. He held onto the horse's mane and squeezed tightly with his legs. Everyone around shuttered at the sight of the Apache in war paint, armed to the teeth like the rest of the men.

The town knew there was a storm coming, but were more afraid now seeing who the sheriff had strung together to defend them. The five horses stood in a line, facing down main street. So far, there was no sight of Paul Harris or his gang.

"Alright, long shot," Durant turned to Delshay and handed him his binoculars. "You and Waltz wait up on the ridge. Keep a lookout for them, they may be coming from any direction."

"Bill," The sheriff continued. "You and Simon wait in the allies on opposite side of the street. When they ride through here, we might have to flank them if they don't take the bait."

"What's the bait?" Simon asked.

"Me," he said.

Waltz and Delshay rode off. Initially, Waltz was leading, but soon Delshay veered off the path and started in his own way.

"Where you going? The trail is up here."

"Your trail. Mine is better," He called back without even slowing his horse. Waltz grumbled and turned to follow. They climbed up the mountain, zig-zagging along the south side. Waltz had never been up this way. He'd only taking his trail that, more or less, spiraled from the south to west to north, back down to south. The old man's horse snorted at the climb, barley having strength to carry a rider over flat ground. Soon, they found a ridge that overlooked the trail leading out of town. Only a ten or so yards away was another vantage point that they could see all of Goldfield.

It looked small to Waltz. The town seemed bigger when he was standing in it. All his problems and paranoia, it only mattered between the streets of the tiny wooden town. But now wasn't the time for reflecting. He checked the sights on his rifle and went back over to the trail overlook.

Durant was in the middle of the street, atop his horse. Behind him stood the mountain and the gold fields. On the other end of main street was the white church, standing apart from the mines and the mountain. It's bell tower and wooden cross stood just a bit higher than any other building in town.

Durant kept his gaze on this building. Beyond it, was the road that led to the Varmint's camp. People had heard the rumor that the Varmints might ride into town and they also saw the signs that there would be a reward for whoever killed Paul or any of his men. So, to the sheriff's dislike, there was an audience of men on front porches waiting with guns of their own.

A small cloud of dust rose up from behind the buildings. Durant started intently as the cloud drew near. Bill and Simon both held their guns tightly, with Durant's expressions as their only que to what was happening.

"A few wagons," Delshay spoke aloud from atop the ridge as he looked through the binoculars. "Couple horses. Nothing else."

Waltz laid down on his stomach and looked through the narrow scope of his gun. From there, he saw Durant take his pistol out of his holster, but the riders heading toward him had no guns visible.

Durant cocked the hammer back on his pistol. His horse hadn't even flinched at the approaching band of riders. At this point, Bill and Simon could read the bold lettering printed on either side of the wagon: THE VARMINTS.

"They really are that bold," Simon thought.

The wagon riders pulled back on their reins and looked to one another at the sight of the sheriff. Between the first and last wagon, Paul Harris was riding on his horse.

"What's going on here, Sheriff?" Paul walked his horse a bit forward.

"I think you know damn well, Paul. I got your poster up all over town. We both know you're not turning yourself in."

For a moment, the air was silent and tense. Flies buzzed between the horses. The riders in the wagons stirred and guns clicked from the crowd, but Durant kept his glare locked on Paul Harris.

"You know me too well," Paul smirked, his hands resting on his two holstered pistols. "I have a deal for you though."

"I'm listening," Durant called back.

"You have someone of value to me. You hand him over and maybe we'll forget about wanting to shoot each other to smithereens."

"I don't know who you think I have. Jail's empty."

"The dutchman that's been hanging round your office lately. Older man."

"I'd hand him over, but I reckon he'll be in the ground soon. Don't know what use you have of him."

"If I say he's Mrs. Thomas's client. Does that mean anything to you?"

Durant sat for a moment. The air felt tight around his throat.

"Make your point, Paul," Durant was getting anxious and so were the men on the sides of the street.

"He's the source," Paul shrugged. "But it doesn't really matter if you think he's valuable. If I'm willing to go away without firing a bullet, then I think that's the nicest deal you're going to get from me."

"I can't just give you one of my citizens."

"That was the wrong answer!" Paul pulled out his dual guns. Durant extended his hand and fired. Paul returned fire, but retreated behind the wagons. From both sides of the streets, men fired into the wagons. Shreds of canvas and wood flew into the streets. Blood and bullets ripping ahead. One of the horses on the back wagon was struck in the neck. The riders inside only had a moment to scream. So much gun fire erupted, that Bill retreated on his horse behind the buildings. Simon tucked behind a barrel and looked out to assess the scene. None of the wagon riders had shot back.

Durant also noticed that no fire was being returned at them. Only bullets fired from opposite sides of the street were firing back at the mob. Durant was the only one with the vantage to see inside. Everyone in the covered wagons had died, and none of them held a gun. He saw Paul retreating to the end of the street, turning back to show his wicked grin, but Durant couldn't ride through the crossfire to catch him.

The whole shootout only lasted a few seconds. Not enough time to fully understand the situation or evaluate what was happening.

"Stop!" Durant heard from behind him. Mayor Weathers ran out into the street, waving a newspaper above his head. "Stop it!"

The crowd on either side of the street ceased fire and looked at their mayor with confusion. Some scoffed. Only Durant felt the cold feeling of guilt. Tears swelled to his eyes.

"What have you done?" The mayor gasped as he walked towards the wagons, shaking at the sight. The canvas was torn and stained. Bodies limp and bleeding over the instrument cases inside.

Durant opened his mouth, but it hurt too much to speak. This was the band called the Varmints. Paul had slipped between them as cover and accomplished his crooked plan to bury the sheriff so thoroughly, that the town would never forget what took place.

"You killed them," Weathers turned to Durant. Even from the top of his horse, Durant never felt smaller. He trembled with rage as he looked around at the men who still held onto their rifles.

"They killed them!" Durant yelled, pointing to the men on the street. "I only fired one shot and it was at Paul!"

"*You* let this happen."

"No!"

"You're done, Durant! I'm telegraphing the marshal's office and reporting that you led all these men to *slaughter* innocent people! You better have your office packed by the time they get here to hang you."

Durant looked around again, the mob of citizens milled around the wagons. If they felt any guilt, they too casted it on the sheriff. They began to yell and jeer, but he couldn't hear a single word they said. He couldn't even see the new cloud of smoke rolling towards the town.

"What happened?" Waltz asked. "They were supposed to drive em this way. What happened?"

"I don't know," Delshay shook his head and put down the binoculars.

They rode back down the ridge and towards Goldfield. The stopped when they saw a stampede of men on horses riding in from the other direction. The two men could hear them firing off their guns and yelling.

"We need to leave," Delshay said quickly. Something must have gone horribly wrong if the men they were set to ambush were now riding through town like they own it. Waltz stared at the scene for a moment.

"We need to go," the Apache said again.

Waltz turned and the two rode away.

Bullets proceeded the Varmints as they turned the corner to main street. The mob that had gathered around the innocent band was now getting flanked by the wave of riders, only picking up more speed. The gang they thought they had killed now stormed at them. Their guns like thunder and lightning, striking down the bystanders.

Durant turned and kicked his horse. Sand flew up as his horse kicked the earth and bullets whizzed past on all sides. One barreled into the horse's hindquarters and Durant was thrown off. He tumbled down onto the gravel, the impact cutting his hands and face. He thought he'd be killed in that moment when he heard a familiar voice.

"Leave him," Paul called from his horse. "Let him rot on his own noose."

The bandits got off their horses and rushed the saloons and stores. They shot Roberto and passed out all the liquor from behind the counter. Some ran up the stairs and broke down the locked doors where the wenches were hiding. Mayor Weathers was still lamenting over the corpses in the street. One rider bolted and kicked him as he past.

"Simon!" Bill called between his teeth. Simon was still crept down behind a barrel in the alley. The two kept their heads low as they went behind the building. They snuck between cover to the end of the street where men firing at the Sheriff's Office sign and the rusty star that hung over the door.

Between shots, Bill and Simon ran inside. The door was partially open with bullet holes continuously forming. Durant was inside, sitting on the floor against the jail cell. Blood ran down his forearms as he buried his face in his hands.

"Durant we gotta go!" Bill ducked as he heard the gunfire behind him. The sheriff didn't move. "Come on!"

Bill grabbed Durant's arm and pulled him to his feet. He didn't let go as he crept to the door and peered out to see if the coast was clear. For now, the Varmints had occupied themselves elsewhere. Bill pulled Durant out the door and back around the office to the alley. They ran and Durant followed numbly. One of the Varmints came around the corner in front of them. Bill threw a hard right and knocked him to the ground. As they ran past, Simon turned and fired back at him.

Bill saw that Waltz and Delshay were no longer on the ridge, hoping to get some cover fire on their retreat. They ran further out of town, away from the screams and gunshots. Eventually they reached the Cholla Corral outside of town. It was empty and quiet.

Durant sat down at the bar. They didn't know where the bartender was, but figured he'd been a part of the massacre.

"This weren't your fault. You know that," Bill said. Still standing to catch his breath. Durant didn't say anything. "This weren't your fault!"

"Yeah, well it certainly feels like my fault!"

"Everyone saw, you only fired at Paul. It was the damned mob that killed those people."

"We'll vouch for you," Simon added, but his voice was doubtful. "Explain what happened."

"Just leave me... Before they string you up too," Durant said, tearing his star badge off his shirt and dropping it on the bar.

"Now, don't talk like that," Bill snapped. "They ain't gonna hang you. Not as long as I'm here."

"We're not fighting the marshals when they come for me! There ain't nothing left, you hear?!"

"You gonna let them hang you?" Simon protested.

Durant sank back and rubbed his face. He didn't know what he was going to do. He could run, but then he'd live on the road the rest of his life. Letting them hang him was the easiest way to be done with it. Just lay down and die was all he wanted to do at that moment. He couldn't bear the thought of what his wife and kid would think when they heard the news. He'd almost forgot about them.

"It ain't right," Simon said, shaking his head. Him and Bill had eventually sat down next to Durant. "It ain't right they're pinning this on you. Now those fucking thieves are still tearing up our town. They ain't gonna stop. But what? Mayor's all concerned about getting rid of the sheriff?" Simon was livid.

Bill was calm, he didn't want to leave, but also not knowing what they could do. Durant reached over the counter and grabbed a stout brown bottle of whiskey. He pulled off the cork and tossed it. He took a pull and handed it to the others. They sat in silence for a while, none of them knowing what to say or do. Hours passed before anyone talked again.

"I suspect people'll probably move on after the dust settles. Can't reckon they'll think it's worth it to keep panning for gold in a town like this. Not while Paul's loose," Bill broke the silence.

"And that's the thing," Simon shook his head. "All this started cause of some gold money."

"Some?" Durant looked up.

"Alright, a lot of money!" Simon yelled; his anger reinvigorated. "It's too much money. We've seen what it does. It twists us. Causes good men to do bad, and bad men to do evil. We all heard Paul. That old man was the miner. He was willing to kill so many people to find that mine."

"I've seen a lot of men go crazy over it..." Bill nodded along. "They kill each other over just a fraction of a fortune. Kill their own friends looking for a mine. *That* mine. Curse it all."

"The money isn't the root of all evil. It's lawlessness. People kill over a claim because they think they can get away with it. People lie and cheat and steal because the west is lawless. Where there is no law, only sin can thrive. That's why they won here," Durant took a pull of the bottle.

"The hell you talking about?" Bill said. "There is law here. There are consequences to breaking it. Now, if you do nothing. You're telling them that they won. But if you pull your sorry ass up and give em what they got coming, and remind them that there is still a star hanging above your door, then they will know this is a town that takes justice seriously."

"You're right," Durant said. He stood up, tucked in his shirt, and put his holster back around his waist. Durant checked the cylinder of his six-shooter to see five bullets left. He snapped it shut and holstered his gun. He took a swig of whisky and then reached out to grab his badge.

"Where you going?" Simon looked up, not expecting them to jump to action quiet yet.

"To bring down the law," Durant pulled the door open and walked out into the night.

The two followed behind. They walked back towards Goldfield, the bright stars glowing above.

Back in town, Paul led the brigade of bandits as they drank as much liquor as they could stomach. They stood on tables and cheered, before falling over. This was the only time any of his men had seen Paul so drunk. He usually stayed sober and kept his head so he could scheme. But there was no reason to now. They had won. They had killed a few dozen people and it was all being blamed on Sheriff Durant. He'd even followed suit with his men and had his way with one of the tavern wenches. No one dared stand up to them now, even if they were drunk enough to have a mild wind push them over.

While the night passed, all the men in the Cantina Roja eventually passed out. They slept on the tables or on the floor. Paul had fallen asleep in one of the beds, but woke up and moved down to the bar before falling asleep again. One of the Varmints got up and staggered out the front door. He doubled over and belched. When he stood and wiped his mouth, three men had appeared before him. Durant reached out and fired his pistol.

The shot woke the men inside. They tried to pull themselves out of sleep, but their heads throbbed and felt like a hundred pounds.

"Take his left gun," Durant said before moving toward the saloon. Durant walked up the stairs and pushed the set of double doors open.

"Paul!" He called sternly. Berns fell off the stool he was on. The men who were already awake sat frozen. Paul lifted his head off the counter. For once, he was caught off guard.

"Durant. Did you come walking in here?" He smirked.

"I'm calling you out, Paul."

"You ain't sheriff no more."

"Then I guess, you should consider this personal," He walked up to him.

"Go ahead then," Paul stiffened up, seeing how serious the sheriff was. "Draw. We'll count how many men kill you."

Durant shook his head.

Berns pulled his gun, but Bill cleared his throat from the doorway. Him and Simon had guns already drawn.

"Just you and me then?" Paul asked as he stood. His shiny guns hung at his hip.

"Just you and me."

Durant backed out of the room. Paul kept his gaze on Simon and Bill as he followed him outside. As soon as Paul stepped through the doorway, Bill reached down and grabbed the gun out of his left hip.

With a shotgun held to Paul's cheek, Bill said, "You only need one."

Paul hesitated.

"Don't tell me you're getting cold feet," Durant called from the street. It was dimly lit by lanterns and fading stars.

"Why don't you just shoot me?"

"Better to let you *rot in your own noose*. This way your men is gonna see I beat you. No games. A fair, just duel."

"Hardly call it fair," Paul's confidence came back as he started to walk down the steps. He knew Durant was right. The Varmints had gathered at the windows. He couldn't let his men see him turn down a duel. "Everyone knows I have a faster draw."

"That won't matter," Durant said under his breath. In his mind, he was worried that it might. Paul had never lost and Durant wasn't known for his quickdraw. He hadn't dueled like this since before he moved to Goldfield. He hoped his aim would serve him better than Paul's speed could serve him.

Forty feet apart, they stood alone on the road. The first light of dawn came over the horizon and met the sheriff's back. Paul's head hurt and the sun peaking over the horizon caused him to wince. His finger tapped on the holster, his hand quivering above the grip. Over the years since he broke his right hand, he'd slowly recovered and the belly full of liquor gave him the confidence that he could pull this off.

The light that rose shown on the town, revealing all the bodies from last night. Flies hovered over them. A dog was in the alley, licking his owner's wounds, not knowing he was long dead. Bill and Simon were tense, not trusting that the Varmints would stay inside and honor the duel. Bill had also never seen Durant even practice his quickdraw and had his pistol ready to kill Paul himself if it came to it.

Durant took a deep breath and slowly lowered his hand to his gun. He tilted his head forward and squinted his eyes, studying his opponent across from him. Paul's hand began to tremble more. He set his hand on the left hip, but knew the gun he needed wasn't there.

Dawn rose and finally, Paul twitched and up went his gun to fire. Durant moved a moment later, pulling his gun. As he heard the gun across from him fire, he took only a second to aim and pull the trigger. The two consecutive shots happened in a flash and Durant was slow to realize the result. He realized he felt nothing and that Paul Harris, with a blank stare, dropped dead.

The Varmints stared out the window as their ruthless leader now lay on the same bloody street as all of his victims. Durant holstered his pistol. People of the town were woken by the gunfire and looked out to see what had happened. What might have looked like another death in a night of bloodshed to some passerby, was really a sign that justice can prevail.

Durant turned to look at all the bandits who were still in their seats. He knew none of them would fire back.

Ghost Town

When the U.S. Marshal's rode in about a half past noon, people had already started to leave town. Just like how they came, they fled in droves and packed all they had onto wagons and mules.

"What's going on here?" A marshal in all black caked from his horse, but no one stopped to answer. "Sir?" They tried again to get someone's attention, but those on the streets moved quickly to leave.

The marshals saw that down the street from them were several covered wagons that were being ignored. The canvas was torn and blew in the wind. Black flies clouded about them, taking off and landing back on the bodies within. The marshals looked at it for a moment before they noticed two men watching them from La Taberna's porch.

"What's happening?" The marshal in all black asked, who seemed to be in charge at this point.

"People're leaving," Bill replied, spitting out some of his chewing tobacco.

"We still have an investigation to conduct."

Bill nearly snorted.

"Good luck getting them to stay. Ain't no one's gonna live here after what took place."

The horsemen turned to look back on the wagons.

"Did you all see what happened? We heard it was the sheriff who shot all them people."

"We heard different," Bill shook his head. "But what do we know, we were over in the canyon. There was a gang supposedly that's held up in there. Sheriff sent us to search it out."

"S'that true?" The marshal asked the other sitting next to Bill.

"That's right," Simon nodded.

"Well, you don't have to hide your stars anymore. Should've just told us you were the deputies around here," The marshal concluded.

"It's a *delicate* situation we're in. Forgive us for being a bit secretive," Bill said.

"I understand. But you two weren't around to see the shooting?"

"Not the first one," Simon answered.

"There was another?"

"This morning, the Sheriff came back out to confront the gang leader he was after, they dueled right about where you're standing," Bill said.

"And that one you saw?"

"Yessir."

"And the leader, this Paul Harris?"

"Shot dead. His whole gang watched him lose and they scattered not long after."

"Where is he now?"

"Well, they dragged him over to the morticians, you could probably see the trail-"

"Not Harris, the sheriff," The marshal grumbled.

"He's in his office, waiting for ya," Simon spoke up again. The marshals turned their horses around and walked them over to the white adobe office. Only now did they see all the bullet holes peppering the town.

"Sheriff," The marshal in black knocked on the door. "Sheriff it's the United States Marshals, we're gonna come in."

"I won't shoot," came from inside. The marshals relaxed their guns a bit and walked in. Durant was sitting at his desk with a cup of coffee. The office was picked up and put back together. Durant's star and pistol were in front of him on his desk.

"We talked to your deputies out there. Seems as though they can't verify what happened yesterday. Apart from you killing Paul Harris."

"Suppose that's what you have to work with," Durant said.

"If only. No, your mayor sent a telegraph saying you led an assault on the wrong Varmint's gang. That you ordered those men be killed."

"He wasn't there either. He only saw the aftermath and jumped to conclusions."

"Be that as it may, that's the only story we have that ain't yours," the marshal walked around the desk and stood over Durant. "For such a public catastrophe, it seems like there's no one that could tell us that you didn't order that killing. And even if you didn't, you surely didn't order it to be stopped."

"I understand," Durant nodded and drained his mug of coffee. He stood up and held out his wrists. The marshal in black grabbed a set of handcuffs from one of his men and cuffed Durant.

They took Durant outside and put him on a horse, securing the cuffs to the saddle. Simon and Bill stood when they saw this across the street. Durant looked over at them, but his face wasn't angry or worried, just solemn. They knew there was nothing left to do, but let him get brunt of the whole mess. He'd killed Paul Harris and I suppose that's what he held onto for comfort.

The marshal in black rode his horse back over to La Taberna and stopped right in front of the porch.

"He'll be hanged tomorrow in Phoenix, if'n that's the thing you want to be there for," the marshal said.

"You sending us another sheriff?" Bill asked.

"No. This town ain't big enough for two," the marshal said and tossed Durant's star to Bill. "Good day," he tipped his hat and rode to meet with the other marshals.

Durant looked back one last time when the horses started off down the trail. Bill tightened his grip around the star badge.

Across town a bell rang. Church was beginning. "How was the church still open?" Bill thought, but it was. All the same. The preacher was in his vestments and stood in front of the ever-shrinking congregation. He read the heavy bible from the lectern.

"And God saw that the wickedness of man was great in the earth, and that every imagination of the thoughts of his heart was *only evil continually...* And it repented the Lord that he had made man on the earth, and it grieved him at his heart. And the Lord said, I will destroy man whom I have created from the face of the earth; both man, and beast, and the creeping thing, and the fowls of the air; for it repenteth me that I have made them...

"And God said unto Noah, 'The end of all flesh is come before me; for the earth is filled with violence through them; and, behold, I will destroy them with the earth... And, behold, I, even I, do bring a flood of waters upon the earth, to destroy all flesh, wherein is the breath of life, from under heaven; and every thing that is in the earth shall die...'

"So ends our reading. My dear brothers and sisters in Christ, God saw the evil of this world. He saw 'only evil continually' and it grieved him. It grieved God so, that he regretted even creating the earth. But what does God do? He destroys it. He destroys evil through the flood. But most of all, he saved the righteous and carried them through the waters. And we ask ourselves, 'who are the righteous?' 'How can I be righteous?'

"Our text tells us Noah did what God commanded. He did *all* God commanded. What does God command us today? To repent and believe in his promises. The wicked are those who do not repent and who do not believe. They are the ones God floods away."

Across the plain, Durant felt the wind brush past his face, riding on a horse for the last time. Yet, he was at peace as if there was no weight on his shoulders.

Deep in the mountain, Waltz was panicky, looking over his shoulder with each swing of his axe. He muttered to himself like a madman, one might have been able to make out the words *gold* and *more* among the incoherent.

"Yet there were other times, God uses water to deliver his people. In the desert of Egypt, God saves Moses and the Israelites by crossing the Red Sea. They walked through the waters as though it were dry land. And Pharoah's army, those with hard hearts were swept away. And again, our Lord Jesus brings salvation through the waters of baptism. He calls himself a spring of living water, and he says this to someone in the desert. As people who live in the desert, we would think it foolish not to go to water. We know better than most how valuable it is. Because of Jesus, we can have this living water. How? Certainly not by building an ark, but by repenting and believing."

Waltz worked his way down the mountain with a sack filled with gold nuggets. The clouds began to darken the sky, like shadowy phantoms floating over the land. They rumbled and rushed. Thunder moaned from within the darkening cloud and with it, rain began to pour. Waltz trudged along, the trail getting slippery and filling with mud. Soon the rain was so heavy, that he had a hard time seeing where the trail was at all. He swore and continued muttering to himself. When he came to the landslide, he slipped and fell down a few steps, landing on his back. His screaming couldn't be heard over the thundering rain. His head swiveled, looking for where his bag of gold had gone to.

"No!" He hollered and forced himself up. He couldn't see it. By now, the sack blended into the rocks and there was no telling where it went to. "No! No! NO!"

But he couldn't find it. Over the sound of the rain, Waltz could faintly hear something else coming towards him. The landslide was starting to slip and erode even more.

"Dammit!" He yelled and ran the rest of the way down the hill and out into the flats. The rocks behind him rolled over each other pushed the debris out further than before.

Waltz peered through the rain to see that the rockslide had been so severe that the entire trail had been covered and could no longer find any way up.

The Waltz heard another sound, a terrible cry from beneath the rocks. But as soon as he realized what it was, the sound was already dead. Horseless, Waltz walked down the trail, coughing in fits and clinging onto himself for warmth. He could feel his pneumonia coming back, but there was nothing he could do but walk through it.

~

Over the next few days, the town began to hollow out. Most everyone had left or made plans to leave. One of the few who held out was Julia Thomas. She'd been anticipating Waltz to come into town to make his regular exchange, but after a week he hadn't shown up.

"He couldn't have left town. He was too stubborn for that," she thought.

After another week, she knew something must be wrong. So, she went out to find his ranch. She knew about where it was, heard of a ranch on the other side of the Salt River where this "old man" lived. Riding there on her mule, it didn't take her long to find the ranch. The door was shut and the windows looked boarded up. Skinny cows fed on what little grass grew along the river. And the stable was empty.

She would have thought Waltz was away if she hadn't heard him coughing from inside. Mrs. Thomas drew nearer and peered through the cracks in the door. A low candle was burning and she could see feet from the foot of the bed.

"Mister Waltz?" she knocked. "Mister Waltz, it's Julia Thomas."

She heard him groan and didn't know whether or not he wanted her to come in, but she opened the door anyway.

"I was worried you might be sick," she said, seeing Waltz held up in his bed. He looked older than usual now. He was thinning and getting weaker by the day.

"Water," he lifted his head off the feather down pillow.

She got up and got him some water. Her husband had been sick with this before he died, so she immediately began tending to him. She lit the wood-burning stove and worked on heating up a washcloth.

"You were out in that storm, weren't you?" she asked, but Waltz didn't reply. He was having difficulty breathing and despite how many blankets he had on him, he was shivering cold. Julia brought him over the warm cloth and patted his forehead with it.

"Waltz, where's your nephew?"

He didn't say anything.

"I didn't see your horse out there either," she continued. He only looked up at her, then started to cough painfully.

"If you want, I can bring your ore into town. Exchange it so you don't have to."

"Like hell," Waltz managed to say. His voice was going. "My gold dies with me."

"What about your mine?"

"That dies too."

Julia could feel that she was getting hot.

"Why you stubborn old man, it won't do you any good once you're gone!"

Waltz grimaced in pain as he thought.

"Fine... But if I," he coughed some. "If I tell you and I do make it out..." His voice was little more than a hoarse whisper at this point. "I'll kill ya."

"You haven't done that yet," she smirked. But Waltz glared at her. The cold glare was interrupted by a fit of painful coughs.

"Through the cave... Past cactus on- on the ledge..."

"Wait," Julia wasn't ready she looked around for something to write on.

"Up and up... Then across, south of the thumb... between the spires..."

"Wait, I don't know where this is!"

"The mountain..."

With that, Jacob Waltz died.

Part 3
The Myth

GOLDFIELD

Thomas's General Store

After Waltz passed, Julia searched through his house. She, more than anyone else, knew how much money the old man had. She tore open his dresser and emptied his backpack, but couldn't find a trace of gold or even a single dollar bill. She thought about opening up the floorboards, but lived in the desert long enough to know what might also be underneath. She turned over the whole house a few times before she admitted that she wasn't going to find anything.

That night Julia Thomas tried to recall what the old man had told her. She paced in the boarded up general store. Her shadow passing along the walls as she circled the flickering lantern.

"Past the cactus... in the cave? No. Through the cave and past the cactus," She mumbled. "Dammit. What was it? Spires and 'the thumb?'"

There were thousands of cacti dotting the mountain and certainly a number of caves. It was too generic. She needed something more specific.

"Dammit, why didn't I look for a map?" She thought about going back to Waltz's house. She thought about going straight to the mountain. The she remembered. She had a map. Not Waltz's, but her own.

She scrambled across the store and went to a case of rolled-up survey maps. She took one and unfurled it on the table. Setting the lantern on one of the edges, the black ink glowed more clearly. The parchment showed an outline of the mountain with the main trails filling the gaps between the names of towns. The map showed all the well-known geographical features. It marked the washouts where people panned for gold, the peaks of the mountain, even the alcove where the Varmints made camp.

Pictures of the land appeared in her mind as she studied the area. She knew what the topography looked like in person. She'd seen these cliffs and stacks from afar. She knew which ones were barren, or covered in sage, or stuck out with a lone cactus.

"Cactus on the ledge," She gasped and dragged her finger to where she'd seen a tall saguaro standing on a ledge, high above the desert plain. The images in her mind served her well, because Julia remembered she'd seen a narrow hole in the cliff just before this cactus.

Her head spung with both excitement and fear. Surely people would know by now that Waltz was bringing in hordes of gold. Everyone heard it at the shooting. And it wouldn't be much later that they would remember who he exclusively traded his ore with. Julia been warned before that the Varmints would be after her, that they made the connection, but none came. Maybe this time, she'd be safe.

"Yes," she thought aloud. "I'll be safe."

Julia turned back from the counter and saw other shadows growing on the wall. She almost thought she was surrounded when she realized what was casting the shadows. Shovels. Picks. Hammers. Cases of dynamite. Julia had everything she needed and she knew it. In the dying candlelight, she gathered everything together. Lastly, Julia pulled out a drawer from behind the counter. In it was a revolver and a box of ammo.

She'd never fired a gun. She'd never even seen Mr. Thomas use one, but kept this one around in case of a robbery. She didn't think about how to use it before grabbing it and tucking it into her waistband.

It had been a few days since the big shooting, and so far, no one had drawn another gun. Julia doubted she needed it, but then again, her only experience with miners was Jacob Waltz and his nephew, both of which were now dead. And she was convinced if Waltz hadn't died of pneumonia, he would have carried out his threat. Regardless, here she was, walking out into the night with a loaded pistol and trembling hands. She walked down the road with her pack over her shoulders. The tools felt awkward against her back and she wondered how the regular miners hauled all their equipment. Maybe she'd learn tomorrow, but tonight she had all the knowledge she needed. She knew where to start and that was more than anyone else had.

Her lantern burned like a firefly floating out of town. The dim light bounced with her steps, but she was sure no one was out awake to follow her. Or to see where she was heading.

The mountain was nearly invisible against the night sky, but as Julia drew closer to the base, she could see the jagged outline. The cliffs slowly revealed themselves as her eyes adjusted. Moonbeams highlighted the ledges and shadowed the caves. One particular pocket looked darker than the others, the light vanishing into the rock.

"That has to be it," Julia said to herself. She scanned the ridgeline and saw the lone saguaro cacti, towering above the valley. She walked closer and saw the washout that had spilled out onto the ground. Even with the heavy bag, Julia was surprising nimble. Her light-footed dancing was something

Mr. Thomas had always admired. But she wasn't thinking about him now. She was thinking about that black cave that that borrowed through the mountain. And what she might find beyond.

She could see stars through the other side. The cave was thin, but now she knew it was passable. From a distance, her lantern had seemingly disappeared into the side of the mountain. Only a very attentive eye would have noticed.

As Julia stepped into the cave, she thought she heard a horse riding out of town, but the twisting walls around her stole her attention once more. Her light reflected off the rock and cast deep shadows at each crux and cranny. She was about halfway through the narrow cave when she heard a buzzing from some type of insect. Looking up, she saw on the ledge in front of her, were two scorpions sitting up on the wall with their tails recoiled. She gasped, hit her head on the back of the wall, and fell down.

She thought for sure she would get stung, but she didn't wait to see if it would happen. Julia pulled her bag along as she crawled out of the cave. Suddenly, she was in an opening, looking over a valley. The Salt River trickled below and reflected the little rays of dawn. She was so relieved to get out of the cave, that she hadn't noticed how close to the edge her hands were. She shuffled back and up onto her feet.

"'Up and up,'" she recited Waltz's instructions. From here, she could see a narrow path that hugged the side of the cliff and snaked up to the flat top. Her legs carried her the rest of the way up. "Across and south of..." Julia looked around, but didn't find what she was looking for. As light finally poured over the top of the mountain, a lot of the hazy silhouettes became clear landmarks. Stacks of boulders, sage brush, and- "The thumb!"

Julia wandered across the flats to the boulders stacked precariously in the shape of a hand with its thumb sticking up. From this point, the ground only became more confusing to navigate. There were spires and needles pointing out of the mountain, but Julia had no idea which ones to go towards.

A shot rang out and a cloud of dust came up from the ground, next to Julia's feet. She turned around, but it was still too dark to see anyone. Her hands fumbled to find the gun she'd brought, and took it out and pointed it randomly at the rocks. She began to sweat and shake even more. Another shot came from the mountain and ricocheted off The Thumb.

Julie spung around and looked for a puff of gun smoke, but she couldn't find any. She pulled the trigger, but nothing followed. She tried pulling the trigger as she waved the pistol in front of her. Before she remembered that she had to cock the hammer, another shot came from the hills.

She ran away from the sound of the gun, leaving her bag of supplies where she dropped it. In front of her, she saw the ground sink down into itself. She could use this small cave for cover, she thought. Ducking down at the sound of another gunshot, she vanished into the ground.

When Julia did finally come out from the cave, she couldn't find her bag. Not even the lantern she dropped, which spilled some of its wax onto the sand. Whoever was up here with her wasn't just practicing their aim, they were trying to stop her. And stop her, they did. She was never going to set another foot on that mountain; certainly, never go looking for Waltz's gold again.

Arizona, 1893

The stories about the dutchman and his mine seemed to fade over the years. In that time, other gold veins had been discovered nearby; ran by companies and deeds. The Bulldog and Black Queen mines brought people back into town. A new generation came looking for riches just like so many before them, unaware of all that proceeded them. Unaware of the ghost that would still linger after them.

In 1893, Arizona became its own state apart from the New Mexico Territory. With statehood, brought reforms. More structured government, more presence of lawmen, and more organized mining operations. There was paperwork and regulations. You couldn't just shoot a man over his claim anymore. You had to buy the whole operation or sell your soul to the company if you wanted a slice.

As the town waxed and waned liked seasons, the only thing that grew steadily was the cemetery. Rows of gravestones marked milestones in this town's history. Some only had first or last names, if they had names at all. Jedidiah Thatcher. Stacy Gray. Dawson. Taylor. "Lucky." Claude: one of our Founders. Mr. Owen: one of our Founders. Wailyn Smith. Mr. Thomas. Big Doug. Hiram: one of our Founders. Anne Redding. Dr. Thorne. Roberto Perez. Paul Harris. Jacob Waltz. Not to mention the host of Peraltas, whose bones lay forgotten beneath the town foundations.

Bill and Simon worked to wrangle up what was left of the Varmints gang. After Harris died, most of them split, but Berns and few persistent others stuck around just to see what more trouble they could cause. They would act like they still owned the town, but as soon as Sheriff Bill showed up, most of them backed down and went home. He hadn't needed to fire his infamous double-barrel for some time. Even in middle age, everyone held onto the image of the ruthless fighter he used to be.

Simon had his fair share, too. He caught Berns going after Mrs. Thomas, convinced she knew where the lost mine was. Simon threw him in jail and waited to see just how high his bounty was before he turned him over to the state. He saw it as a fitting end for the reckless rebel, having to endure a slow due process that would be worse than death.

But that God-forsaken mine was a memory that wouldn't go away. Even as time marched on, the pair found more and more people asking questions about the old dutchman; where he lived, where he worked, who he worked with. Bill would tell people to drop it, but eventually all the questions led to Julia. At first Mrs. Thomas started selling maps just to get people to stop harassing her for information. That didn't last long though. Like everyone from the "old days," she left, not wanting anything to do with it anymore.

Delshay would join the sheriffs every now and then, when trouble was looking to outnumber them. They corned a few highwaymen who were responsible for a long streak of robberies. The bandits had their backs against a cliff wall and fired all the guns they had to stay alive. Bill had snuck around to flank them, but one of the bandits had the same idea. Bill had turned to fire, but this young buck had the quicker draw.

Simon and Delshay finished them off, but it was too late. By the time they go to Bill, he was dead. They searched all the bandits, but found them nearly empty handed. They had no gold or cash. All they found was a stone with a carving in it. A carving that resembled a cactus on the side of a cliff. Delshay left it with the rubble and went to help Simon lift Bill onto his horse.

As Simon became sheriff, he tried to steer people away from the lost mine, but the rumors only drew more people in. Yes, many panned for gold and worked for the companies, but every once in a while, one of them dared to find it. People search all sides; all faces of the Superstition Mountains. Most turned up empty handed if they turned up at all. Stories were spung from survivors recounting their tales in saloons or as witnesses shared around the campfire. Stories about a lone horseman chasing people off the trail. Or of an unseen gunman high up in the rocks. Some even claimed it was the ghost of Jacob Waltz, trying to stop anyone from finding the lost mine.

Yet these reports were never taken seriously by Simon or any official after him. They stayed as they were: only ghost stories.

Ghost Stories

The turn of the century brought the turn of another page in the Goldfield story. Industrialization was on the horizon. Trains brought more people to Phoenix, which took the mining town's population. Settlers and prospectors moved on to what was bigger and better, leaving behind only a few hollow buildings at the base of the mountain. A sheriff's office, two saloons, and a church. It wouldn't take many years to for the sand to fill in the washouts and mines. All of the ghost town's progress would be covered up by time. And for many years, Goldfield went forgotten.

The town would have stayed off the map, if strange reports didn't begin to resurface. In 1931, a treasure hunter by the name of Adolph Ruth went missing in the Superstition Wilderness Area. When they found his remains, there was a hole in his skull where he'd been shot and killed point-blank. The cracks supposed formed an X in what remained of his frontal bone. It took another year for hikers to find Adolf's pack. Inside was a journal, covered in sand.

I found it! I followed the map and found it! It was incredible! Just like the stories said, "across the flats, in the "heart" of the mountain." Veni Vidi Vici!

But when the hikers looked in his pack, the map was gone. Along with everything else. They reported this to the Goldfield sheriff's office, but it was dismissed as a closed case. With no tangible evidence to continue. In their official report they said that Adolph had broken his leg while hiking in the Superstitions and while he was bleeding out, he simply hallucinated finding the mine. They made no mention of the hole in his skull.

Eventually his son, Erwin Ruth, went looking for the mine, knowing that his father really did have a map. He knew his father had survived many treacherous expeditions and knew this was no accident. While turning over clues, he met someone named Pedro Gonzales, who said his mother's maiden name was *Peralta*. The son of a treasure hunter and a descendant of the original owners would be the perfect team to find the lost mine. They made plans and drew maps, but before they had even set out, both men went missing.

A few years later, a group of surveyors came across a row of skeletons. The skulls each had an X shaped hole through them. The sheriffs came up from town and took the bodies away, but no autopsy was ever released. When the surveyors tried to go back to work, they were told that the whole area was now under investigation and they'd have to move on.

In the 1940's another journal was found by an unsuspecting hiker:

He's here in the mountains. The killer. It's him, who's been making all these people disappear. He shot at me when I was reaching the top. I would've died if I'd gone any further. I must have been close. I knew it was-

The rest of the page had been torn out. On the other side of the page, it continues:

I tried to back that night. Thought that I could sneak closer. I even saw a lantern up where I was earlier. It has to be him, Mr. X...

There was silence around the mine until about 1960, when George Conrad Mueller claimed to have found it during his trip to Phoenix. The Superstition Mountains weren't far away by car and many went out to see them and visit what was left of the historic ghost town. Before George had time to lead a group back there, he was reported to have died of a heart attack.

A couple in the 1980's took their honeymoon hiking all over Arizona. They made plans to see the Tortilla Flats, the Superstition Wilderness, Meteor Crater, and hike down and up the Grand Canyon. They checked out of their hotel in Phoenix before heading East to tour the Goldfield Ghost Town before heading out to their hike. But they never checked in to their hotel in Flagstaff that night. The claim was reported to the Phoenix police and the Pinal County Sheriff's, but their investigations were inconclusive.

Stories like this surfaced more and more. Many accounts being recorded in newspapers and stored in library microfilms. As time went on, these stories started to coalesce and form into the long-running superstition of Superstition Mountain. Locals and tourists alike became fascinated by the legends, and the mysteries that seem to overshadow the area to this day.

Florence, AZ, 1990.

Rob Briant sat at his desk with his boots propped up. He was humming along to a Marty Robins vinyl, that played softly from the record player. He had grey hair and bristles along his chin. His eyes were tired and he let himself rest them for a moment.

"Sheriff!" Kenneth Conner walked in. Briant opened his eyes and stared at Kenneth as if interrupting his peace and quiet was worse than whatever situation was going on outside.

"What, Conner?"

"There's a car up past mile marker 7. Pulled off by the Service Road."

"It's not illegal to park there."

"It's the car we marked yesterday, sir. The white Corolla."

Just then, Briant dropped his feet from the desk and grabbed his hat. The easy smile went away from his face. He pulled open the gun cabinet and topped his pistol off with bullets.

"Have your gun?" he asked Kenneth.

"Yup," the young deputy reached into jacket coat for his concealed carry. Lastly, Sheriff Briant grabbed the gun that had been hanging on the wall above his desk.

They fled the brick building and jumped into their own squad cars. The two Dodge Chargers burned down the road. The sirens roared and the red lights boiled as the cars disappeared into a mirage. They pushed eighty, ninety miles per hour when they turned West on the Superstition Freeway. Briant's eyes followed the mile markers as they flew by. 12... 11... 10... 9... 8...

Briant swerved onto the service road at Mile Marker 7. He fishtailed when the car went from asphalt to gravel. A dust cloud shot up and not a second later, he was hit the gas pedal and shot like a bullet toward the parked car at the end of the road.

Kenneth Conner was only a couple seconds behind him, driving on the side of the trail of dust that the sheriff kicked up. They rolled up the hill, the dirty white Toyota just ahead, the mountain stuck out just beyond.

Briant's car had hardly came to a stop when he stepped out with his gun pointed out. Kenneth took his time and went to the passenger side of the dirty white car.

"Now, you best come out with your hands up!" Briant ordered. They could see the driver inside stirred a little. The man looked back over his shoulder, but the squad cars blocked his retreat. The driver opened the door and donned a face of panic.

"What the hell man? I didn't do nothing! You can't do this!" His face was sunburned and covered in sweat.

"He's armed," Kenneth said calmly, noting the holster on the man's left hip.

"Now, we just have a couple questions for you and I'm sure we can all go on our way."

"What's going on?" The man was shaking and his arms were starting to lower.

"Keep those hands up!" Kenneth ordered, tightening his aim on the suspect.

"What's in your car?" Briant asked.

"Wh-what?" the man replied.

"Stop messing around, what equipment do you have in your car?"

"Just, uh, a metal detector."

"Just that, huh? Why don't you open your trunk?"

"Am I doing something illegal?!" He asked.

"Keep those hands up," Kenneth said again, the man lifted them back above his head.

"I said open your trunk, son."

"Alright! Shit!" The man slowly went back to his open car door and with one hand, slowly reached for the lever to pop open the trunk.

Kenneth moved quickly to the rear of the car and lifted the trunk. A shovel and a pick.

"Can you explain this?" Kenneth asked, pointedly.

"It's just a shovel, man. It ain't illegal to carry one!"

"But it's illegal to dig out here. Everyone knows that."

"I didn't," the man pleaded.

"Bullshit. Your plates were flagged. You've been out here before," Briant stepped in again.

"It ain't mine," he said quickly. Briant's eyes narrowed. "Shit, I mean-"

"So, either you're just that stupid to admit you stole a car or you're lying to me and you were about to go digging around in government protected land. Which one do you want to go in for?"

"It ain't illegal to hike out here, is it?" the man quickly asked. "I'm just going for a hike. I'll go right now. Leave all my stuff right here," he started to take a few stepped back. He nearly tripped over the chain that drooped between the fence posts, blocking off the service road from the desert ahead.

Briant holstered his gun. Kenneth followed suit. They watched him back up before turning around and walking quickly into the wilderness area. Briant went back to his car and put on his Stratton hat and grabbed the gun that he'd taken from the wall mount.

"Go back to the station," he ordered.

"But-"

"Conner," Briant shot him a look.

"Yes, sir."

Kenneth Conner went back into his squad car and turned off the flashing red lights. He backed up and turned to roll back down to the road. He checked the clock on the dashboard: 3:47. It took him a moment to realize what he was late for.

"Of all days..."

Quickly he sped back down the road, down to Florence. When he got there, another car was parked out front. He hurried inside and brushed his hair back in place.

There was a man immediately inside the door. He had the same deputy's uniform that Kenneth wore, except this man's shirt and pants were ironed, unstained, and appeared exactly up to dress code.

"One day in the field, and your uniform won't look so good," Kenneth walked past him. This man was larger and older than Kenneth who had only been a deputy for a few years.

"I've been in the field for ten years," the man corrected, now looking down at Kenneth's sloppy appearance. "Deputy Mason Taylor," he grabbed and shook Kenneth's hand.

"Uh, Kenneth," he replied.

"Where's the sheriff? He was supposed to meet me hear at Three-thirty."

"Ten years in the field, you might have learned we have to take a call every once in a while," Kenneth shook his head. He grew up in Florence and had always held himself above his classmates for becoming a sheriff's deputy. But this outward ego was only compensating for his truly low self-esteem.

"Listen, if we're going to work together, you need to check your attitude," Mason kept a straight face. He had a strong jaw, freshly shaved. He looked down at Kenneth without so much as lowering his chin.

"It won't hurt if you relaxed some," he replied. Mason dropped the subject, seeing that he couldn't go anywhere.

"You said Sheriff was on a call?"

Briant panted as he climbed boulder after boulder. The yellow rock radiating the dry desert heat. Sweat dripped from the brim of his round hat and evaporated as soon as it hit the ground. Less than a hundred yards up the mountain was the man they'd confronted.

The man looked back over his shoulder, but never saw anyone behind him. He kept going, up and around the stacks and the infamous "jumping" cholla cacti. He worked his way up the mountain, turning every now and then. He still saw no one, but this far up the mountain, he could see his car with the Charger right behind it.

"Shit," he knew he was being followed. He drew his pistol and kept on.

Briant squinted as he looked up, the sun was now low enough to be in his eyes. He tried to shield the light as he surveyed the cliff above him. Just then, a small rock was knocked loose and skipped down the cliff. His eyes darted to where it came from. Briant's chest filled with nerves. For a moment, there was nothing.

Then a shot rang from the ridge and Rob Briant could hear the bullet ricochet off the rocks at his feet. He immediately drew back behind a boulder. Silence followed. Briant peered over to see the ridge. His hat was shot off his head.

"Jesus!" He shrunk lower behind the boulder. There was a line of rocks that Briant crawled along to stay out of sight. At a new angle, he peaked out from cover. He could see the man now, whose head was also exposed as he looked for his enemy below. Briant held his pistol steady on the rock in front of him and fired. He hit the man's arm. Briant could hear him swear and run further up the mountain-side.

Briant ran after him, staying low as he wound up the trail. He followed the track of blood to an overlook. When he found the man sitting on the ground, he holstered his pistol. The sheriff then took hold the extra gun he'd brought with him, removing the strap from around his shoulder.

"Why the hell do you care if people are up here digging around?!" The man yelled at Briant, squeezing his arm to try and keep himself from bleeding out.

"It would take a long time to tell ya," Briant said and fired. The echo carried over the mountain, scaring the blackbirds below.

~

Rob Briant walked back into the sheriff's office. He looked tired and his arms were full of different equipment, a metal detector and a pick.

"Sheriff Briant? Deputy Mason Taylor," Mason was almost blocking his way and went to shake the sheriff's hand, but Briant moved past him to the evidence locker.

"A pleasure... Conner! Get this thing opened."

Kenneth shot up from his seat with a large set of keys. He fumbled to find the right one before unlocking the steel cage that sat in the back corner of the small office. Briant dumped the equipment in the locker and left it there.

"'Mason,' you said?" he went for his desk.

"Yes, sir."

"You transferred here from Detroit?" Briant asked, half paying attention.

"Dodge City, sir."

"Well, close enough. You like the heat?"

"I can stand it fine."

"Good. You're gonna need to. Nothing but hundred-degree days for a week."

Sheriff had been informed only last month that he would be getting a second deputy, despite him always insisting that two men could handle the job. So, neither him nor Kenneth were really enthused on his arrival.

"That gun," Mason pointed to the empty mount. "The plaque says it's a William Moore & Company. Must be pretty old. Does it still work?"

Briant looked to Kenneth before answering.

"Hardly. She's more of project. I take it in to get cleaned every few weeks."

"Hmm," Mason grunted and looked to be taking a mental note.

When the office was closing for the night, Briant noticed that there was still another car in the parking lot with him. He'd been the last one to leave by at least a half hour. The yellow street light cast a shadow over the person sitting in the car. Sheriff Briant could see this man was talking to... to himself, it looked like.

Mason hadn't noticed he was being watched as he clicked stop on his tape recorder and quickly drove off. Mason drove out of town a ways, up towards Phoenix, and stopped at a dark roadside motel. Neon pink glowed into the parking lot from what was left of the sign, and it mixed with yellow sconces beside each room door. Mason locked his car and walked swiftly up to the second floor. The night air was still hot, but other than the flies around the streetlights, it was quiet.

He looked out over the balcony before unlocking his door, which ever hung a "Do not disturb" sign. He entered the black room and turned to lock his door again before flicking the light switch. On one bed was an open suitcase with uniforms and a change of clothes, all pristinely folded. The TV was removed from the dresser and it was instead used as a desk, with a host of newspapers and microfilms.

From his jacket, he took out a cassette recorder and set it on the dresser, where he'd eventually set his keys and eventually, his pistol. Then, Mason took out a flip phone and extended the antenna before dialing. It rang only once before there was an answer on the other line.

"Agent Phillip Anderson reporting in," Mason said before hanging up and stowing the phone away.

He took off his uniform one piece at a time and meticulously folded them before setting them in his hamper. The only time he relaxed his shoulders was when he fell asleep.

Pinal County Sheriff's Office

Mason had arrived to the office before Sheriff Briant, which was a habit the middle-aged man was getting tired of. Mason took off his coat, folded it, and set it down in one of the waiting chairs. It had been a month since Mason transferred in, but he was still bootcamp-stiff. Kenneth, as always, was just a few minutes late. Mason had given up on scolding him for this daily discrepancy. And at this point, Kenneth had accepted that indifference was the best he could ask for from the stone-cold officer.

Briant had poured himself a cup of coffee and took in the moment of peace.

"Sheriff," the ham radio behind the desk crackled to life.

"Son of a-" he grumbled under his breath. "Yup," Briant picked up the mic.

"There's a crash down on 87, near the correctional center."

"We'll be there," Briant said before taking one final gulp of his coffee.

Sheriff Briant got in his own car, while Mason rode with Kenneth. They went west out of town and turned south on highway 87. They flipped on their red lights and sirens. It might have only been three minutes, but to Kenneth, the ride with Mason felt like an eternity. If he was in the car any longer, Kenneth feared he'd have to resort to telling jokes in order to pass the time. Though every intuition in him said that Mason had no humor. Kenneth probably would have made fun of him for being so uptight, but Mason had twice the muscle and at least six inches in height. Luckily, he saw Sheriff's brake lights flash and pull to the side of the road. Kenneth slowed to park behind him. Immediately, Mason got out of the car and went to examine the scene.

There were black marks on the road where a small truck had spun in a complete circle, leading their eyes to where it crashed into in guard rail. The second car, a 12-passenger van, was further down the road, past what was left of its own fender. The drivers of each car were standing somewhere in the middle.

"How could you not see me? I was driving right beside you!" The man yelling was burly with a bushy beard and rolled up plaid shirt.

"*No se que paso! No-*"

"Alright, what's going on?" Briant walked between them.

"I was driving the speed limit, when these people sped by, but before they passed me, they swerved into my lane!" The driver explained furiously, pointing back to his small pickup. A few cars slowly went by on the far side of the road.

"Is that true?" Briant asked the Mexican man, standing in front of his family.

"*No entiendo. Éramos-*"

"In English..." Briant rolled his eyes and looked to the five of them standing there. "*Habla Inglés?* Anyone?"

"*No Inglés.*"

"They cut me off!" The burly driver started again. "Caused me to spin and crash, they're paying for this!"

"I think we heard from you," Rob Briant said and looked back to the family. "Licenses?"

Their expressions went blank.

"Do you have your driver's licenses?" he asked again, but they didn't move.

"Sheriff!" Kenneth called from his car.

"What Connor?"

"There's a call for you over dispatch."

Briant left them for a moment and went back to his car. A muffled voice came from the ham radio inside.

"Sheriff?"

"Yeah?" Briant answered.

"We have a call from some college kids, apparently their roommate never made it back from his hike yesterday and isn't picking up his phone," the radio had a short click of static before going silent.

"Did they say where he was hiking?"

After a moment of nothing, there was static and then the muffled voice came through again.

"Yeah, looks like he was heading out on the Peralta Trailhead."

"We'll go up there, thanks."

Briant put down the corded mic and looked up at the two deputies.

"Conner, why don't you go up there and see if you can find him?"

"With all due respect, sir," Mason spoke up. "In a search, more people make a more efficient sweep."

"Alright, fine," Briant said quickly. "You go with em, but if I'm still busy cleaning this up when another call comes up, you're taking it."

"Yessir," Mason said and followed Kenneth Conner back to their car.

The two up the county road, passing back through Florence, crossed over the dried-up Gila River, and hooked a right on highway 60. They drove past several dusty service roads before finally turning at a sign marked: TRAILHEAD. Mason was rigid as they drove. He was annoyed they were only going the speed limit, but it didn't take them long before they reached the abandoned parking lot.

There were only a few sandy cars on the cracked pavement, the whole area surrounded by saguaro, cholla, and bur sage. Kenneth and Mason walked out from the lot and started down the trail. They moved past the sign that pointed toward the Peralta Trailhead.

"If he's lost, wouldn't he be off the trail?" Mason asked as they walked.

"You bring up a lot of objections for someone who's still new in our unit," Kenneth shook his head. "Most times, they're not far off the trail."

"Doesn't it bother you that it's not being taken more seriously?"

"What isn't?"

"People going missing. This is twice now since I've been here. First the owner of that White Corolla and now this college student."

"Statistically, people go missing in national parks and wilderness areas more than anywhere else. Guess it doesn't surprise me that people get lost," Kenneth looked up and saw the distinct outline of the Superstition mountains in front of them. The green cacti standing out from the warm hues of the earth.

"So, you're not worried about this guy?"

"No. I'm not. Look, people get lost, even if we don't find em, they eventually turn up."

"Most of the time."

"Yeah, most of the time."

They walked up the trail further and got to where the Peralta Trail splits from the one they were on. They veered off and slowly starting climbing the sloped landscape.

Mason scanned the ridges above them.

"I'd look down," Kenneth broke the silence. "People've been known to fall into pits and break their leg. They can't stand and see how close they are to the trail."

~

After clearing things up with the car crash, the Sheriff made his way back to the office. He picked up his antique gun from the where he dropped it off to be cleaned. Then, he mounted it back on the wall above his desk. The small brass label below it was fading, but it was easy to see what kind of gun it was. It was a break action, shotgun from the late 1800's. It had two long barrels, each with their own hammers. It had been passed down from sheriff to sheriff for a hundred years.

It had been the custom to give antique western-era guns as gifts to many of the law enforcement around the state. So, no one thought twice about it hanging above the sheriff's desk. "It was out of use," so far as everyone thought. "Simply a trophy item," but Briant and Kenneth knew it was much more.

~

"All I'm saying if there's a serial killer up in these mountains, more should be done about it," Mason hadn't left the subject. Him and Kenneth still hiked the dry yellow trail that curved around the base of the Superstition.

"There isn't a serial killer living up in here."

"Decades of disappearances, bodies have been found with gunshot wounds or worse. One would think the law would be doing something about it."

"Do you know how often this area is searched? For missing hikers or whatnot?" Kenneth replied. "It's a lot. Arial footage would show if there's someone living in a tent or shack."

"Okay, maybe they don't live in the mountains, but that's where they always kill. Always this mountain."

"And I suppose you're the one to find them? A serial killer who leaves no evidence."

"Except bodies."

"Well, if the FBI or whoever wants to look into it, let them. We have enough on our hands, looking for lost hikers. We can't go chasing ghost stories."

Mason was quiet after that. They worked their way up the rocks, looking back on the high vantage points.

~

Briant looked across his desk to the chair Mason had set his coat on. He looked around, knowing no one else was in the building, then got up and walked over to it. He checked to pockets on the bomber-style coat and found nothing, but he felt like something might have been further inside. Turning the jacket inside out, Briant reached into the inside pocket and pulled out a tape recorder.

He walked back to his desk and pressed play.

"October 13. Agent Phillip Anderson. Got a look better around at the office while the Sheriff Rob Briant and Deputy Kenneth Conner were away. All appeared normal except for the missing gun above the desk. By the plaque, it looks to be a double barrel. Late Eighteen-hundreds. Matches description of murder weapon in multiple cases. Sheriff said it's 'out of order,' but brings it to be cleaned regularly. Note: go to gun cleaners and ask if it looks like it's been used...

"October 14. Only a day since I've been here and already there's a missing persons case. I went out to try and find the lost hiker while the others were out on a call. I followed the tracks out from his car. It looks like the man was followed, but I lost his trail as soon as they reached the rocks. My request for an arial search was denied.

"November 2. The small staff and hesitation to the transfer of my alias, 'Mason Taylor,' adds to the case that the they are trying to keep their activities more contained. Even after some time, they are still hesitant to my presence. Note: Deputy Conner is relatively young and inexperienced. I might be able to get him to talk if I get a chance with him alone...

"So far, the murder weapon is the only tangible piece of evidence that could be reported back to the FBI. However, the long history of mishandled cases regarding disappearances and murders in the Superstition Mountain region all point to the conspiracy that the officials are-"

Briant clicked the tape off and slammed the recorder onto the desk. He stood, took the cassette tape out of the recorder and put it in his pocket. He reached back at the wall and grabbed the mounted shotgun, and left the station.

Mr. X

"Conner, what's your twenty?" Briant buzzed over the walkie-talkie strapped to Kenneth's vest.

"Bout half-way up the Peralta Trail. No signs of the missing hiker," he responded. Mason was a few paces away, but listened in.

"I'll meet you two at the top, near the mouth."

"Sir?"

"Just go there. I'm on my way," Briant snapped. The walkie buzzed for a second, then went silent.

"What was that about?" Mason turned.

"Sheriff's on his way, he's gonna help us search," Kenneth lied.

"Should we wait for him?"

"No, he said he'll catch up," Kenneth didn't look back as he kept on. He could feel himself getting jittery. Luckily the hundred-degree heat covered how much more he began to sweat.

"You're picking up your pace. Everything all right?" Mason called ahead, starting to get on edge himself. If he was right about his suspicions, then he knew what he was in for.

After what felt like another hour, Kenneth swerved off the trail and started on another unseen path, steeper now up the arid rock, but going back toward the direction they came.

"We'll get a better vantage from up here," he said quickly, looking around to see if he could spot the Sheriff's car.

Mason had his hand on his holster as he followed. They moved up to a small ledge, one that overlooked the surrounding desert, with the sun just beginning to sink into the afternoon. Kenneth looked back down over the ridge and saw that there was another squad car next to his.

"Shouldn't we stop here? This overlook seems as good as any," Mason suggested.

"Good idea," Kenneth gulped the lump in his throat. "Gives Briant some time to catch up."

Both men pretended to scan the area below, but always kept the other in their peripheral view. Mason was torn between actually finding the missing hiker and preparing for the worst. He didn't want to end up as the next missing body out in the wilderness, but even then, he knew if he didn't report in at night, the FBI would be alerted.

Kenneth began walking again. Without a word, Mason followed. They zig-zagged up the mountain and came to a flat area towards the top. Kenneth kept walking straight across, between the stacked boulders. Mason knew they were no longer looking for the missing person and unbuckled the strap of his holster. The two walked until they reached a cave that borrowed straight into the mountain.

"I'm sorry," Kenneth turned around.

Mason had pulled his pistol, but it was too late. Briant had appeared from over the top of the boulders and fired nearly point-blank. The double-barreled shotgun roared and the echo could still be heard by the time Mason's body hit the ground.

~

"We won't have much time," Briant burst into his office, with Kenneth right behind him. He dropped the antique double-barrel shotgun on his desk. "Feds'll be here."

"The feds?" Kenneth asked, looking around horrified.

"They're onto us. Mason was giving them intel. I found a recorder in his jacket."

"Could we run? Could we-"

"No. You can't run from the feds. Not with what little resources we have. But it ain't no use. We'll be caught, we'll get the chair. We're through, Conner. Through!"

"Could we explain it to them?"

"What?"

"Could we tell them why we did what we did, why we *had to* do what we did?"

"If we told them everything—and I mean the whole bit—do you think they would see it as just? Do you think they'd see it the way we do? They wouldn't understand. They'd rather leave it up to fate to stop people from finding that mine..." Briant took a few deep breaths before continuing. "Sheriff after sheriff, we've been trained to do our duty and stop anyone from going after it. That it was better to kill the source then to let the bloodshed get out of hand. It's a classic debate of morale and I thought that the answer was always clear."

"It is clear. I still believe that. If all you've told me about the history of that mine is true, then this is what we needed to do. Cut the head off the snake before it gets loose. There needs to be a Mr. X, there needs to be that necessary evil holding back the storm. That's what you taught me!"

"You're right," Rob Briant picked the shotgun back up. He broke it open, seeing the chambers were empty. Snapping it shut again, he handed Bill's old weapon over to Kenneth. "It's up to you now."

"What?" The young man looked pale.

"I told you Mr. X was a necessary evil? Then it's of necessity he stays alive. I'll turn myself in. Say the mantle ended with me, that you were too young and that Mason was too rigid to train." Briant moved to the gun cabinet and took out several small boxes of shotgun shells and a few boxes of 9mm bullets. He stuffed those into a duffle bag and threw it on his desk. "Now, you take these and whatever else you'll need and you go to the mine. You stay there."

"And do what? If I'm hiding, they'll know I'm involved."

"You just stay there and write," Briant pulled out a ream of paper from his desk and dropped it in the bag. On top of that, he set the typewriter that had been on his desk for at least a decade.

"Write? What are you talking about?"

"Right now, the feds have their own narrative of what we've been doing. Maybe they won't come to see it as we do, but someone needs to hear the whole story. They need to know what we were trying to stop. Write it all out. Only come down when it's done. Mail it off to the state courthouse. Publish it, for all I care. That'll be our defense."

"I can't let them just take you," the young deputy lowered the shotgun. "I was a part of this just as much as you were!"

"You listen to me," Briant grabbed his shirt. "You get yourself out of here. I'll take the hit. That's an order," Briant pushed him towards the door.

So, I did. I took the duffle bag and drove my own car out to the service road past mile marker 7 and pulled off next to the white, sand covered, Corolla. I threw the duffle bag over my shoulder and hiked up the jagged-topped mountain. The city of Phoenix looked like a mirage in the distance, blending with the vapor steaming up from the ground. Between the mountain and that hot city was a dinky, wooden tourist attraction called Goldfield.

I had been there a few dozen times, and read all the books on their "history" as they presented it. I knew the truth. The truth had been passed down from sheriff to deputy for generations. I knew that evil was at work from the very beginning. Maybe a remnant of evil still lived up in the mountains. Maybe it was the devil, maybe it went by the name "Mr. X," or maybe men were just evil. Whatever it was, it was alive and well in these mountains.

At the mouth of the mine, I set my typewriter down and leaned my shotgun against a nearby boulder. And then I wrote. Maybe someone out there would understand our cause, or maybe we're just putting ourselves out there to be judged in ethical debate. Whatever people come to think of us, the truth of that mine and the strongest warning to avoid it must be preserved. No one should ever go looking for it. Don't risk the greed, the malice, the bloodshed. Yes, we killed to stop killings. We shot first and buried our dead. But if we hadn't? I can only speculate how many more would have died.

Of course, I changed the location of the mine. It's too dangerous to reveal where it really is. I need to ensure that no one can read past these warnings and take the directions given. Sure, the government could go back and search for everyone involved, try and track down every witness. They could try and use arial footage and radar to find out where this mine lies. They could check all the facts and read all the newspapers, turn over every Peralta Stone, and find the tangled history of murders and rumors to discover what was really going on here. Or they could admit that this case is very simple. That there are only three people involved:

The mine, those who died going after it, and me,

Mr. X.

ARNTSON

ACKNOWLEDGMENTS

This work of historical fiction is not meant to depict real history. Although historical people appear in this novel, their personalities, actions, and motives are purely fictional. For further reading on the history of the Lost Dutchman's Goldmine, there are dozens of books, articles, websites, and documentaries on the topic.

The following are all the events and situations in the novel based on events that have or rumored to have taken place:

1. Miguel Peralta was a real prospector who is supp-osedly the first to have found the mine and left cryptic maps of stone behind.
2. The most western battles of the American civil war in Arizona, such as the Battle of Picacho Peak and Apache Pass, really happened. And the victors of those battles are as recorded here.
3. John C. Cremony (who was in the battle of Apache Pass) really did write his account with the Apache and released the first Apache-English dictionary;
4. Dr. Thorne was supposedly led under blindfold to *a* gold mine after he aided a wounded Navajo;
5. Three confederate soldiers did try and get information from Dr. Thorne for supposedly knowing where the

lost mine was, though this likely didn't take place in Goldfield;

6. Jacob Waltz, a native from Germany, was a rancher and supposedly found a "Peralta Stone" leading him to the mine;

7. Jacob Waltz did call on his nephew to help with the mine, and in turn killed him in fear he would spill its location;

8. Julia Thomas did sell mining equipment to Waltz and tried to get the location out of him upon his death. She also sold fake maps to the mine after she tried and failed to find it;

9. The mysteries surrounding the mountain in recent history are also based partly on facts, as hikers have gone missing as recent as 2009, including Adolf and Erwin Ruth and the journals mentioned with them, though the journals are not direct quotes;

10. Another journal mentioned a "Mr. X" as the serial killer living in the Superstition Mountains.

Obviously, I don't take lightly the murders of real people in history nor do I actually believe the local officials have anything to do with such cases. Again, this is a work of fiction, based on the cloudy history of a western gold town and the rumors that live on to this day. If you would like more information, you have but to look up any of these points online and follow the same rabbit hole that I did. Then, let your imagination run wild.

Open-source images courtesy of the Library of Congress
Cover image courtesy of Dave Cotton

Sheriff, 1936

Cowboy, 1898

Apache, 1903

Superstition Mountain, 1917

Surveyors, 1917

Salt River, 1910

Gold Miner, 1907

Geronimo, 1890

Grand Canyon, 1910